Edward A. Robinson

The Disk

A Tale of Two Passions

Edward A. Robinson

The Disk
A Tale of Two Passions

ISBN/EAN: 9783337413866

Printed in Europe, USA, Canada, Australia, Japan

Cover: Foto ©Andreas Hilbeck / pixelio.de

More available books at **www.hansebooks.com**

THE DISK;

A

TALE OF TWO PASSIONS.

BY

ROBINSON AND WALL.

.

BOSTON:

CUPPLES, UPHAM AND COMPANY.

1884.

CONTENTS.

CONTENTS.

PART II. — THE EFFECT.

CHAPTER IV.

CHAPTER V.

CHAPTER VI.

CHAPTER VII.

CHAPTER VIII.

CHAPTER IX.

CHAPTER X.

CHAPTER XI.

Part I.

THE CAUSE.

THE CAUSE.

CHAPTER I.

MESSRS. HAMILTON AND REHKOPF MEET, AND, IN
TALKING OVER PAST EVENTS AND FUTURE PROS-
PECTS, MENTION THE NAME OF JOHN ALDER.

IT was the fifteenth of September, late in
the afternoon.

The tremulous atmosphere, which all day long
had been vibrating between the walls of the
tall buildings, still clung to the broad thoroughfares.

In the money-changing parts of the great
city the streets were almost deserted.

Finance had put up her shutters an hour
ago, and at this moment, perhaps, was swing-
ing in some rural hammock.

The sun had been too hot for fashion also,
and those who had already returned to town
from their summer outings, kept to the cool

houses, so that, looking up Grand Avenue from the Stock Exchange, neither in the immediate foreground was there any stir, nor yet, farther on, where the broad, smooth street passes out from between bank buildings and the like into the realms of fashion and becomes the beautiful promenade.

From the far-away distance on the left came the indistinct roar of trade.

Over there were the wharves, the warehouses, the mills, the railroads, etc.

But here, that roar had dwindled to an echo merely, which had a quieting effect on the people in the *cafés*, who sat fanning themselves and chatting at the windows, and on the strollers who sauntered aimlessly by on the walks under the lengthening shadows.

Among these strollers are two young men, who hold important parts in this narrative.

Mr. Albin Hamilton, tall, fair, intelligent ; but careless in dress and motion.

He is sauntering up town, evidently without knowing why or wherefore.

A block or so away, from an opposite direction, comes Bernard Rehkopf.

Rehkopf is the opposite of Hamilton, almost ; of dark complexion and painstaking in attire.

Rehkopf is always busy, too, never careless of time.

Now, though he is walking slowly, he is evidently walking somewhere and, withal, his mind is busy.

These two young men were chums at college, but separated since graduation, now some five years ago.

In the early part of their college course, Hamilton once saved Rehkopf's life : pulled him out of a hole in the ice.

Whenever Rehkopf tried to express his appreciation of the deed, he found that Hamilton would not listen to him, and he himself was more inclined to show his feelings in deeds than in words.

As a result, he stuck to Hamilton like a brother, providing in his cool, practical, common-sense, that balance which the other lacked, and, unperceived, steered his friend through many temptations to excess, especially dangerous to a man of Hamilton's temperament.

All this time they are approaching each other.

At length Hamilton sees the other, and rushes with his usual impetuosity to meet him.

Then follow the hand-shakes, the slaps on the back, and the excited, broken ejaculations, that seem to say little, but express so much, and it is some time before they recover from their surprise and get down to connected discourse.

"What are you driving at now, Al?" said Rehkopf.

"O, I was strolling about the streets in the state of mind of ancient Micawber."

"That is to say, you have nothing to do," said Rehkopf, seizing his friend's arm. "Come to dinner with me and we'll talk it over."

It was agreed, and arm-in-arm they crossed the street, and entered Katesby's, where, taking seats at a table in a cool, secluded corner, they made preparations for a cosey chat over the events of the past five years.

When the waiter had departed with their orders, Rehkopf, regarding his friend for a moment in silence, began : —

"Do you know, Al., old boy, you knocked me

completely out, appearing when I least expected
you; but you have n't altered a bit as far as I·
can see. You are the same careless, witty,
brave fellow that " —

"Hold on, my friend, that's enough of that.
Those were brave old days, though. If we only
could live them over again, but " — with a shade
of sorrow in his face — "we can't, and such
meetings as this of ours to-day have always an
element of sadness in them; at least for me.
Now I notice how fast time has flown; but
what upsets me is, that I see no successes;
nothing gained but a subsistence; no name,
no wealth to any great extent. Let 's see,
the last time I saw you was at the Cring-
stone station. You remember, don't you? and
how we promised to keep up a correspondence,
and " —

"And it fell through," interrupted Rehkopf,
with a smile.

"Yes, and other plans have fallen through,
too," muttered the other.

"Oh, come now, brace up, you're too blue by
half; you can't expect to upset us all in five
years. Come, give us some idea of what

you have been up to.   How are you fixed now?"

"Oh, I've money enough for the present, if that's what you mean, but otherwise I'm a dead failure."

"What's been the matter?" asked Rehkopf.

"How shall I answer that, I wonder.   Ever since I left college I've been drifting about from pillar to post; at one time State Assayer of C——; at another chemist and instructor at the Institute of Technology; then assistant electrician to the Great Northern Electric Motor Company; leaving each position to follow some will-o'-the-wisp that promised better, never sticking to any one thing long enough to become indispensable to it, and, of course, never accumulating any money.   Besides, I am convinced that I am fitted for something; and, if I can strike that, I can make a success of it. Now, I am trying to make up my mind what I had better do next; resolved, that if I get into anything, I will stick to it, no matter what tempts me to quit.   There you have it; now it's your turn."

"Well, I have little to say.   I am no failure,

nor yet a brilliant success. I have stuck steadily to business and worked out something, but I 've had no great opportunities as yet."

"Now I should think, to a man of your abilities, life would be one grand opportunity for pecuniary success ; and I suppose that 's what you 're after. This is such a speculative age, and so many new discoveries have been and are being made, that it seems to me, a man with your business training might very easily become connected with some big enterprise ; or, better still, organize a company for the purpose of handling some great invention or discovery. Chemists and electricians are constantly developing new things, and some of them contain wonderful possibilities."

"That 's all well enough ; but where are these chemists and electricians ?"

"Everywhere. I know hundreds of them. Some studying in one direction, some in another, some of them going over the whole scientific field with a comprehensive sweep, taking in everything, and evolving wonderful ideas more or less practical."

"Considerably less practical," remarked Rehkopf.

"Now, you 're wrong there ; the ideas are all right ; in fact, I don't believe there ever was anything invented that could n't be turned to practical account by the right man. The fact is, inventors — so to speak — are one-sided geniuses ; they never know anything about practice, and never are able to make a practical, money-getting use of their discoveries. They keep to their study, satisfied with just enough to live on, and to keep themselves supplied with material for experiment, seemingly content with the results they produce in a scientific way. They make a discovery, sometimes reduce it to practice, but oftener leave it undeveloped, to chase some new idea or suggestion, which never profits them anything. I know of one man in particular whom, if I had your business tact, I could use to good advantage."

. "Who is he ? "

" John Alder."

"Who is he, and what is his brilliant invention ? "

" Don't be sarcastic, Ben. The more I think of it the more I become convinced that there 's your grand opportunity. To begin at the beginning : when I was State Assayer, three years ago, an old man came to me for information as to the best place to find a certain mineral. I did not have the desired information at my tongue's end, so promised to look it up for him. But he did n't leave just then, and both of us soon became interested in conversation. I found him immensely entertaining and very deep in study, and learned that he was away from home and staying in C—— to investigate the peculiar characteristics of some of the minerals there. In leaving he gave me his name and invited me to call. I took advantage of the invitation, and there made the acquaintance of his daughter Mabel — a most charming girl. Well, it was n't quite the old, old story, but something near it. If I only had money — but that's foreign to the subject. After awhile he left C——, and took her with him. But she and I have kept up a correspondence ever since, and when I came here the other day I called, — for they live on the outskirts of this city, — and there had a glimpse of the old man's ability. But this was in the afternoon. Mabel entertained me, because Mr. Alder was busy, so I did n't see much of his work. When I came to leave, however, he remarked that he would like, sometime, to show me a device of his, for the transmission of almost anything, any distance, except heat."

"O bosh! do you believe him?"

"Now, I don't know. You can't tell. He is a born inventor and thoroughly read in all the departments of science; better not make up your mind in advance, but let's go and see him."

"Then you think there is something in it," said Rehkopf.

"'Twill do no harm to see him, at any rate."

"When shall we go; to-night?"

"Let's get his permission first. He's queer, and might not be in a communicative mood if we dropped in unexpectedly."

"See him to-night, then, and try to make an appointment for me. Does he have many callers?"

"No; Mabel tells me that no one ever comes there from one month's end to another. The people are so curious, like to gawk and stare and wonder, ask so many stupid questions, and so generally annoy and interrupt her father in his studies and experiments, that he will have none of them. Then they gossip about him, I suppose, tell all sorts of queer stories concerning him, and take a peculiar delight in watching his house ; they hear strange noises ; see great volumes of smoke and steam escape from the chimney by day, and fire by night ; they do not understand an inventor's devotion to his work, or his horror of annoyance ; so they persist in their gossip and watching. O no, he has no visitors. They regard him as altogether too difficult of approach."

" Quite a character, is n't he ? "

"Yes, he is, indeed," replied Hamilton, "and one well worth studying from a business point of view."

" Glad to hear you talk about business, Al; we will see Alder and find out what there is in him and his discoveries to interest capital. But now 's the time; we must take things on the run in this age. Is he connected with the Central Telephone office, do you know ? "

" He is in the suburban circuit, but we ought to be able to reach him from the central office. I did n't think of that before. If you're through dinner let 's go over and see."

Together the two friends hurried to the central telephone office, where they were informed that they could be put in communication with any of the patrons of suburban lines.

"Ring up John Alder, Centreton, please:" said Hamilton to the attendant at the switchboard.

Then followed the usual calls to the different stations, until the official, with a little more animation in his voice than usual, said :—

"Is this John Alder, Cliffs, Centreton?"

*   *   *   *   *

"Well, wait a moment, here 's some one who wants to speak with you."

Hamilton took the receiver.

"Hullo!"

*   *   *   *   *

"Hullo!"

*   *   *   *   *

"O, it 's you, Miss Mabel, is it, I 'm Hamilton!"

Then followed a little conversation, unimportant to this narrative, until Hamilton broke in —"But what I would like to know is, whether your father will be in a humor to receive visitors this evening. I have a friend with me, inter-

ested in science, who would like to talk with
him."

*   *   *   *   *

" Well, I wish you would."

A longer silence followed, during which Hamilton stands staring on vacancy and holding the
receiver to his ear.

Once more he starts to life.

" Hullo ! "

*   *   *   *   *

" He will ?   Well, we 'll be out between half-
past eight and nine.   Good-bye."

CHAPTER II.

ON THE ROAD TO JOHN ALDER'S.—THE STORY OF ALDER'S LIFE.

HALF-PAST SEVEN found Rehkopf and Hamilton in a dog-cart just leaving the city, with ten miles of smooth country road between them and their destination.

Hardly had the wheels ceased their rattle over the pavement, when Rehkopf began asking so many questions with regard to the life and character of John Alder, that Hamilton saw no way of satisfying him, except by telling him all he knew about that gentleman.

"All I know," began Hamilton, "about Alder and his history, is made up from hints and broken threads of conversation, which I have picked up, now and then. Such sources are unreliable, but he has been a study for me, and if he could be induced to give you the particulars of his life himself, I am reasonably sure they would coincide with the ideas I am going to give you.

"Somewhere between fifty and sixty years ago, there came a great rejoicing into the family of a certain Enoch Alder, over the birth of a son. This Enoch Alder was a chemist by profession, and lived in a pleasant cottage on the outskirts of one of our large eastern cities. He was connected in some way with the government of that city, but for his leisure hours, he had fitted up a private laboratory at home. In this cottage he lived for years, caring for no one but his wife; passing what time there was left him from his city work in his own laboratory. No wonder that there was great rejoicing over the birth of this child, for Enoch and his wife lived a secluded life, far from all their relations. The boy, though slender, proved healthy and flourished. When he became old enough to creep about, the dangerous things of the laboratory were removed beyond his reach. And that room became his playground. The sun shone into it, and the father, passing a part of his time there, loved to have the boy with him and to watch his childish wonder at the strange-shaped things

about him. As the child grew older and began
to take notice of his father's work, he, too, caught
the spirit of the place; built his furnaces from
blocks in imitation of his father's; and, over
imaginary fires, carried on his childish experiments. He absorbed a love for chemistry
almost with his mother's milk, and lisped about
nature's indivisible elements at a time when other
children take to nursery rhymes. He went to
college when the time came, and it came early,
for the boy was bright and quick to learn.
While there, he made few friends, and no reputation for general excellence, but in chemistry
he was at home; and, in his room, which must
have been the haunt of horrid smells, he origi-
nated, now and then, some startling effect, that
electrified his class. Although he graduated low
down in rank among his classmates, he carried
with him into life, great skill and an unwavering
devotion to a single branch of science; prophetic of his success in the future.

"Soon after he left college, his father, the
great friend and teacher of his youth, died,
leaving him alone — for the mother had passed
away when he was a child — and at the mercy

of the world, to which he was comparatively
a stranger. He had no relations, no friends.
About him he saw happy homes and laughing
children, while across his threshold no foot ever
came save his own. He made up his mind to
marry, and having a comfortable property which
his father had left him, found it a matter of no
great difficulty. Somewhere, somehow, he met
a lovely woman. They were married, but soon
discovered themselves badly mated. He had
seen in himself, with alarm for the future, a
growing devotion to one thing, and care-
lessness of aught else. He had thought that,
with a wife to brighten and to cheer him,
his heart would warm to human interest; but
he did not change. He found that there was
no room in his heart for anything but his
work.

"She was deceived; for she had thought that,
in her husband's home, she would find sympathy
and encouragement, and that out of the admiration she really felt for him, love would grow.
But, when she entered his house, what little
brightness there had been in her young life
began to fade, and over her a darkness spread

which never disappeared. She found herself in an untried situation, where she had duties which must be learned; where there was much to dis courage her; and when, in her new trials, she looked to her husband for help and consolation, she read in his cold, speculative eye the story of a mind, which, careless of her, was following the zigzag road to fame.

"After a time a child was born, a daughter; and the wife hoped that the cloud which shad-owed her would break and pass away. But it did not break, and as the child grew and began to look with seeing eyes, it turned to the father and watched his motions with wide-eyed wonder. A stranger came across the path of this unhappy woman. She fled with him, leav-ing her child. Alder awoke, when too late, to find his wife flown, and a little, toddling child stretching out its hands to him for comfort. Then, I think, he realized his own shortcomings and took most of the blame for his wife's fault on himself. The deed had been committed; it could never be undone, and he steeled his heart to endure the inevitable. Yet, with it all he was just, and in his soul registered a confession

˙ that he was the most to blame. The child was
left, and into her life he poured his small stock
of warmth and affection; growing up, she
showed a character which joined the affection-
ate warmth of her mother with the inquiring,
analytical spirit of her father, so that, under his
care, she grew to love him, to like his work, and,
despite her years and sex, to be in some meas-
ure a companion for him. Just when he came
to this part of the country I have never heard
him say: probably soon after his wife left
him."

"That's a sad history," said Rehkopf, "but
how does he act with strangers?"

"Well, that's easily told," responded Hamilton; "talk with him five minutes, and the conversation will flow easily into a discussion of
chemistry and electricity. With regard to his
discoveries, he will probably be uncommunica-
tive, but I think that, in time, he will show us
˙ something of his work; and I am sure that
there you will find something of practical use,
consequently of pecuniary value."

"But why is it you yourself have never investigated it?" asked Rehkopf. "O — but come

to think of it — you have never had the chance,
have you?" saying which, Rehkopf lapsed into
silence, and the conversation afterwards turned
on other subjects.

At length, Hamilton turned in from the
main road upon a broad avenue, that had evidently long since passed into disuse, for the
grass grew rank there, and there was scarcely
a trace of wheels. Along this they sped noiselessly.

"This reminds you of the primeval forest,
does it not?" said Hamilton, pointing to the
great elms and maples that raised their arms
aloft, motionless in the still air, casting shadows
black as midnight on the meadows and grass-
grown roadway.

"I don't see much of the forest," responded
Rehkopf, "but England, to my fancy, should
look like this."

"And so it does, very like," said Hamilton.
"Now all this land must have belonged at one
time to the man who occupied that grand, old-
fashioned house you see over there through the
trees. No one lives there now, however, and
Alder's servant says it is haunted. I can't help

thinking that that old house exercises some influence over the fortunes of Alder. Why, I don't know; unless, perhaps, its location and the air of mystery which hangs over it have something to do with it."

Soon, however, they left the house, with its ghosts, behind them; and the horse, reducing his pace to a walk, began a steep ascent, which ended suddenly in an open plateau.

On the opposite side from them stood a long, low, gambrel-roofed house, with barns and sheds attached, appearing in the uncertain twilight as if they were sadly in need of repair.

" There is our hermit's abode," said Hamilton.

" Well, I don't see anything remarkable there, save fine opportunities for improvement, and a most culpable neglect of them."

Hamilton, who was familiar with the place, tied the horse under one of the sheds, and then they approached the house together. Light came streaming through the windows of the rooms on each side of the doorway, but the door itself and its immediate vicinity were black as Erebus.

The old-fashioned knocker was vigorously applied, the door was opened, and Hamilton and Rehkopf entering this temple of promised revelation and mystery, followed the old servant through a curiously lighted, low-studded hall into a sitting-room, and found themselves in the presence of John Alder and his daughter Mabel.

CHAPTER III.

JOHN ALDER: HIS HOME, HIS DAUGHTER, AND HIS
INVENTIONS.—A WONDERFUL LIGHT.

THE furniture was old-fashioned, but as hand-
some as that of more modern manufacture.
There was a large sofa of most comfortable
proportions, covered with dark red velvet, and
furnished with pillows and foot rugs, which
would have satisfied a sybarite. Quaint, old,
easy, and three-cornered chairs, with stamped
leather seats and backs, were scattered here and
there ; while the oak floor was covered with
Persian rugs, old and faded, but of the richest
quality.' The window hangings were dark red
velvet, and through a partly drawn *portière*
Rehkopf saw a corresponding luxury in the
arrangements of an adjoining bedroom ; he also
noticed that, like the hall, these rooms were
lighted in some mysterious, unknown manner.

When they entered, Alder arose from one of

the easy chairs to receive them. Rehkopf found himself in the presence of a tall, well-built, but spare man, of about sixty years, clothed in a long, loose-fitting house coat of dark color ; on his head, which must have been quite bald, he wore a skull-cap of the same dark-colored material, from under which thin, straggling locks of hair descended. The face — that is to say, the part left uncovered by the long, white beard — bore out most accurately the character of the man. It was colorless, bloodless, but not pallid ; the nose straight and well-bred ; the eyes deep sunken, dark, and penetrating, were set far apart. The expression was kindly, but firm : while in the heavy, partly lifted, partly contracted brows, there resided a look such as must come into the face of any man who handles habitually the dangerous forces of nature, and watches for the results of untried experiments ; results which may place wealth and power in his hands, or blow him to the moon.

After the introduction of Rehkopf, a word of pleasant greeting from John Alder and his daughter, Hamilton briefly stated the object of their visit, and requested Mr. Alder to show

Rehkopf something of the results of his studies in the science of electricity.

"Come to my workroom, then ; I can talk with you best there," said Alder.

He led the way across the hall into an apartment that occupied fully one half of the lower floor of the house, and was evidently used as laboratory and library combined.

Here were furnaces, retorts, crucibles, mortars, flasks, jars, electric batteries, coils of copper wire, metals of various kinds, chemicals and acids of every description, arranged around the floor or upon shelves, while a large and well-filled library of scientific works occupied the whole of one end of the room. A large table, littered with open reference books and papers covered with memoranda, also held a prominent position in that part of the laboratory. The whole thing seemed mysterious and strange to Rehkopf. For here again was that same peculiar light, which he had noticed in the hall and sitting-room, and which did not appear to come from any particular source, but was diffused and cast no shadows. The atmosphere seemed filled with a luminous matter, the particles of which were inconceivably minute and projected fro some unseen source with a velocity equally : conceivable.

Rehkopf was more than surprised. He h seen a great many devices for the comple illumination of a room, but never anything li this. He had been connected with all sorts schemes for arc lighting, for incandescent a for portable lights, operated by storage bat ries concealed in the base of the lamp; but ne had he imagined the possibility of a light l this, that seemed to be continually pouri through and filling up every nook and cor of the room.

There was no doubt in his mind, without a further examination, of his ability to place t discovery on the market, and create a sensat such as had not been known for years. But it patented? Had anyone else been operat in the same direction? Could it be possi that John Alder had discovered and had b using this light for any length of time with the knowledge of the world? Hamilton assured him, it is true, that aside from him and Mabel, John Alder saw no one. This was

enough in its way, but the inventor was a strange
man, one naturally calculated to arouse something more than idle curiosity among his neighbors ; and Rehkopf knew that in every place
there are always people to be found, people
ready to take advantage of and appropriate the
results of others' thinking. With these and
similar thoughts flashing through his mind Rehkopf said : —

"This is a remarkable light you are using
here, Mr. Alder. I never saw anything like it
before. Is it one of your own inventions ? "

" Yes."

" How long have you had it in use ? "

" Perhaps six months."

" Have you ever taken out a patent for it ? "

" No. I am not satisfied with it."

" I don't quite understand where the light
comes from."

" It comes from the walls and ceiling."

" Do you use it altogether ? "

" Yes ; it is the same in all the apartments of
the house."

" Will you explain the nature of it to me ? "

" Certainly. A metallic base is covered with

a kind of paint prepared from chlorophane and other materials, and brought under the influence of an electric current, whereby it is gently heated, and throws off a luminous matter, which floods the room with light."

" Is it expensive ? "

" On the contrary, it is comparatively inexpensive, but it is not permanent. The effort necessary to produce the light causes a gradual waste, and the walls and ceilings would have to be repainted every year or two."

" But it is vastly superior to anything else known, and if it is produced at a nominal cost, why not get out patents, and produce it to the world? There is money in it."

" Perhaps it might be well to do so if I had nothing better; but I have succeeded in perfecting a still better method of lighting, which, after the first cost, would last for an indefinite length of time, requiring no attention whatever. People soon tire of anything that requires attention, and demand something better. This reason, combined with the fact that my last discovery contains every element that is desirable, all that humanity could wish for, has prevented me from doing anything with this light. This is an age of production and discovery, and inventors are always striving for something better."

"Yes, I know," interrupted Rehkopf, "and it is this growing wave of production which fills me with uneasiness. There is money in everything new that is of any practical benefit to the world, and — you will pardon me — it seems to me that unless you have already something practical, I cannot urge upon you too strongly the importance of securing this. Great works are asked for, but it is time lost to undertake the improvement of any invention that is in itself far in advance of what the world now possesses. I think it is a good plan to make the most of what you have, and I cannot understand why you have not long ago submitted this invention to the public."

"Because," said John Alder, "I would have to pay too dearly to get their favors. A man belongs to himself only while he is unknown. Hardly are you welcomed by the public before you become its slave. Had I gone to the public with the light you now see, I should have been overwhelmed with insatiable curiositymiongers, and have had no time for the development of a much better, less expensive, and more natural light."

"Will you show this new light to us?" asked Hamilton, quickly, just in time to prevent some sharp remark from Rehkopf, who appeared out of patience at what seemed to him Alder's dilatoriness.

"Yes, what is the nature of it?" asked Rehkopf, a little more calmly than Hamilton had expected.

"O, simply a reflected light," responded Alder, "conveyed over a wire from an illuminated station. It may be from a station lighted by the ordinary arc light, or from one where the sun is shining."

"But is this possible?" interrupted Rehkopf. "Can you conduct light over a wire?"

"I know it is as possible to transmit light waves over a wire by the aid of the electric current, as it is to transmit sound waves. Also that this discovery comprehends a principle that will control the future of telegraphy, or, more properly speaking, teleoptography."

"Do you say," said Rehkopf, "that you can

transmit light from one point to another over a wire, and use that same device for the transmission of intelligence?"

"I cannot say that I have been the first to discover the principle as it might be applied to the transmission of intelligence, but undoubtedly the first to use it for the purpose of producing light."

"How do you apply this principle?" asked Rehkopf.

"By controlling all the rays of light and bringing them to a focus upon a sensitive plate, which, under the influence of these rays, becomes intensely electrified. A wire thence leads to another plate that might be removed to any distance. Now, whatever I expose to the transmitter, be it light, a landscape, a horse-race, any scene, in fact, or any message whatsoever, from a half dozen words to the whole side of a newspaper, is all registered on the delivery-plate, and remains there until the circuit is broken. If I wish to have light only, the transmitter is exposed to the sunlight, or any well-illuminated station, and the seleniated delivery-mirror instantly responds, giving in quality an intense light, which it would be necessary to pass through a diffuser before it could be made available for general purposes."

"Pardon me, Mr. Alder," said Rehkopf, "if I seem incredulous, but what you have stated is so radically new and startling, that while there may be perhaps a principle here that could be developed after a time, the accomplishment of it for the present appears altogether too difficult for us now to waste time in experiment over."

"There is no experiment necessary," said John Alder; "the thing is already accomplished."

"What!" cried Rehkopf, thoroughly aroused; "can you show me a working model of such an instrument? something that is at this moment practical?"

"I can," quietly responded Alder; "but only over a short circuit; from one room to another."

"That will be sufficient; if it will work over a short circuit, it will over a long one; electricity annihilates distance."

"I will show you what I have done, then," said Alder.

He then placed a small, polished disk upon an easel and connecting it with the wire leading to the sitting-room across the hall, broke the circuit connecting with the walls and ceiling, when, with the exception of a small circle of light coming from the disk, the room was in total darkness. Through the medium of this disk, as through a small aperture, one seemed to be looking into another room, where, in the soft, mellow light, the furniture and the hangings were distinctly visible. Mabel, too, appeared, seated in an easy chair, and busily engaged upon some sort of needlework, unconscious of the interested eyes that were watching her movements.

"You see," said John Alder, after a few moments' silence, "how perfectly the model works, and that, too, with a light having comparatively no actinic power ; of course, with a direct light, the result would be much more satisfactory."

"This is wonderful," said the two friends, in a breath.

"It is worth millions of dollars," continued Rehkopf ; "it does everything but speak."

"It will do that, too," said Alder, "for I

have succeeded in making the disk sensitive to sound. I would show you that, also, but my coils have been unwound and they are necessary. I am sorry I cannot demonstrate it now, but I have already made use of that feature, so there is no question about it whatever."

"Mr. Alder, I am more than satisfied," said Rehkopf, thoroughly impressed with thoughts of the future for such an invention. "I thoroughly believe you. What you have shown us almost passes belief, but you should keep it as secret as the grave until you have covered it with letters patent from every country on earth. This should be attended to, and at once. I have seen all I wish to for one night."

CHAPTER IV.

IN WHICH ALDER, HAMILTON, AND REHKOPF LAY THE FOUNDATION OF A GREAT STOCK-COMPANY.

ALDER, closing the circuit, and relighting the room, took a chair near the two friends and sank into it like one tired by an exciting exertion, the fire in his deep-sunk eyes dying slowly away.

There was silence for a moment. Hamilton saw, or thought he saw, a brilliant future for himself in connection with this invention, but he felt that he had done all he could for the furtherance of that object, by bringing Rehkopf and the inventor into communication with each other. He had confidence in Rehkopf's judgment, and believed that if there was anything for their advantage in helping Alder develop the invention, he would see it, and bring it about in some way. Now, relieved from all responsibility, and having the rare good sense to see that the best he could do would be to keep silent, he leaned back in his chair, with half-closed eyes, dreaming bright dreams of the future.

Rehkopf was hard at work in his mind, mustering his forces. He comprehended the magnitude and possibilities of the invention, saw this grand opportunity, saw, too, that Alder was fast losing his interest in the present, slipping away into the unrealized dreams of his imagination; and made up his mind that if he would make any impression on him, he must begin at once.

So he said, — "I am a young man, it is true, Mr. Alder, and what I am going to say may seem unnecessary to you, so much my senior in understanding as well as years. But I have been kicked about in the hard school of experience for some time past, and there I have learned to know an opportunity when I see one. It seems barely possible to me, that you have kept a discovery of such importance in your mind, even having reduced it to a practical certainty, without taking steps to put it upon the market, and securing the advantages of its development to yourself and family."

Rehkopf all the time felt sure that nothing
had been done ; still, at this crisis, he was not
free from the fear that what Alder might be on
the point of saying, would sound the death-knell
to his hopes. Sitting bolt upright in his chair,
he held his breath in expectation. The importance of the moment had its effect on Hamilton,
too. But he said nothing, and sat motionless,
watching Alder with eager eyes.

Alder spoke at last, but neither his tone nor his
words expressed any excitement, or any feeling
on his part that affairs were drawing to a crisis ; -
simply as a man who had accomplished a result,
and was now making some unimportant remarks
on details.

"I have always had a consciousness that there
would come a time when these things would
have to be reduced to practice. As yet, however, I have done nothing, except to secure myself by patents, against theft, and I have never
had a reason — at least, so it seemed to me —
for doing so. I have money enough for all my
needs, while, on the other hand, whenever I have
demonstrated an idea to my own satisfaction,
something always lingered like an after-glow,

which, if carried out, promised me better results, higher praise. I knew that if I stopped to make money, all progress in the direction of the new Idea would be hopeless. Lately, since my success in this invention, though I have given the matter a more serious consideration, I find that my life and education have placed difficulties in my way. In youth, I mingled little with those of my own age; self-assertion, and that sharpness which boys acquire, in their youthful battles, which both protects them from one another and helps one to control the others, I never acquired. Then, too, the experiences of my later years, some of which have been painful enough to me, though uninteresting to others, have carried me farther and farther from the paths of men. So you see me now, without friends, whom I can trust, and, excepting you two, almost no acquaintances whom I might learn to trust."

Alder stopped; his voice holding the same even pitch to the end. But in his meditative eyes there lay the traces of the struggle going forward in his mind. Was he looking back on years spent in steady, brain-wearying toil,— years productive of great results, but results

which he had no power to control ? did he not
see, besides, that from his devoted years all the
bright lights of happiness had passed away ? was
he not sad, disappointed, and, without knowing
it, in the best condition possible to take on the
influence of Rehkopf's strong, practical mind ?

"But we are no nearer a determination," said
Rehkopf; "the thing seems to hang fire. What's
to be done ? "

"As you see," said Alder, wearily, "I have
tried to determine on some plan, and finding
none, have concluded to let the practical development of the invention depend on chance; to
let things drift on as they have been doing."

"But, Mr. Alder," said Hamilton, taking a
sudden part in the conversation, "this drifting
is purposeless; it does not bring you out anywhere."

Another pause. Then Rehkopf, with more
determination in his voice, asked:—"Mr. Alder,
you would be glad to see this invention on the
market ? "

"Yes. I know it would be of use to the
world. I feel that I owe it to my own reputation. If money were my sole object, however,

I would take no part in it. Of that I have '
enough and to spare for my simple wants."

" Yet, as I understand it," said Rehkopf, "you
would enter into no plan that would bring you
in contact with the public."

" No."

" But how can you avoid that?" said Hamilton, impatiently, as he started from his chair
and began walking up and down the room. The
conversation seemed to him to be moving in a
circle.

" Wait a bit; I've been thinking of a plan,"
said Rehkopf, and, leaning forward with his
elbows on his knees, he emphasized every point
of his argument with the motion of his hands.
" Suppose for a moment, we three joined in the
development of your invention, Mr. Alder?"

" Well?"

" How could we work it? In the first place,
it would take us years to establish it on a pay-
ing basis, if we were unassisted by outside
capital."

Alder sat meditatively, biting the ends of his
beard, and said nothing.

" Money must be borrowed," continued Rehkopf, "and a stock company is the best way to do it. No one will lend money at the small legal rate of interest, for any purpose, where the risk seems to be great to him. Everyone who takes great risks, wishes the possible profits to be proportionately large. So, for their money, they must have an interest in the concern."

" Yes ! " assented the others.

" Now, I have had experience in forming companies. I know all the men about town who would be likely•to take hold of an infant enterprise, and I know that I can make them see that there are advantages for them in taking hold of this. As financial manager of this invention, I will guarantee to place it on the market, form a company, and have twenty-five million dollars in the treasury to start it in good order ; throwing in my time, and borrowing enough money on my own security to arrange for showing the invention to a number of capitalists, so that they may see what it really is. That is agreeable, as far as it goes, is it not ? "

Hamilton said nothing ; he was beginning to fear that his part in the future was to be small.

"Yes," said Alder. " But who will superin-
tend the mechanical part ?"

" I was just about to speak of that," continued
Rehkopf. "An invention so thoroughly scientific, and of such delicate construction, requires
of the chief superintendent devotion, skill, and
experience. You would be unwilling to attempt
it, because it would bring you in contact with
men, and in Mr. Hamilton you have an excel-
lent substitute."

" Yes, certainly," muttered Hamilton, overcome by the change his prospects had under-
gone so suddenly.

"I find no objection to that," said Mr. Alder.

" Now," said Rehkopf, " how shall the interest in the invention be divided between us and
the company ?"

Alder, after a moment's thought, said, slowly
measuring every word, " If you, Mr. Rehkopf,
will take the management of the financial, and
you, Mr. Hamilton, of the mechanical part, and
if you will agree never to try to bring me into
connection with strangers, never to mention the
place where I live, I will give you a three-

quarter interest, which you may divide as you see fit."

Rehkopf, suppressing all traces of excitement at the munificence of the offer, said, "That three-quarter interest had better be divided, at least for the present, as follows : one third to you, Mr. Hamilton ; one third to me ; and one third to those who are to become stockholders."

So it was agreed, and Rehkopf, taking a seat at the table, wrote out an agreement for the others to sign.

Meanwhile, Alder and Hamilton talked over in a low tone the technique of the invention, and the former, warming to his subject, gave the history of it, and arranged for the latter to come to the Cliffs daily, — to live there, if need be, until he had mastered all its secrets.

Soon afterwards they left for town. Little was said on their way back, but the nature of their thoughts, as they drove homeward in the moonlight, can be easily imagined.

At Rehkopf's lodgings they separated, agreeing to meet next day to lay plans for the exhibition of the powers of the photo-electrophone.

CHAPTER V.

TWO MONTHS LATER.— REPRESENTATIVES OF THE
PRESS AND CAPITALISTS ARE ENTERTAINED.—
THE DISK VEILED.

Two months have passed since we saw Rehkopf and Hamilton driving away from the
Cliffs; two months of work and worry. On
the next day they met as agreed, arranged their
plan, and divided the work.

Rehkopf took upon himself to provide sufficient money for the test, and to select and
work up what men he thought best calculated
to take hold of the invention.

Hamilton immediately packed up his belong-
ings, and left for the Cliffs ; there to study the
invention, and fulfil his part, finding in Mabel
an enchanting companion for his leisure moments.

These two months have been so well employed by Hamilton and Rehkopf, that this

pleasant afternoon finds them awaiting the *dé-nouement*, their preparations all complete. .

A room has been hired near the centre of the city, and fitted up sumptuously. Through the parted draperies the declining sun is casting a few lingering beams, which fall on the white cloth and glittering ware of a table, set and waiting for the banquet and the guests.

The caterer and his men have departed, leaving Rehkopf and Hamilton together. The latter can be heard moving about behind a curtain that hides a part of the room, while Rehkopf paces slowly up and down by the side of the long table, his hands deep in his trousers pockets, and his face set in meditation.

At last Hamilton appeared from behind the curtain, his face beaming with satisfaction, and, walking up to Rehkopf, broke into his reverie with a hearty slap on the broad shoulder, and the remark, "Now, old man, I'm all ready; what are we to expect from you to-night?"

"We are to expect representatives from all the newspapers; I have made considerable impression on the managerial mind, and in every case the best man will be here. Then, too,

every one is correspondent for papers i
large cities, and you may be sure th
scenes we are to enact to-night will be r
millions of people before to-morrow's :
Among the capitalists come, first, Bob
and Harry Van Dyke, representing be
them one hundred million dollars. Bo
these are young men, with adventurous s]
and, besides, have confidence in me. I e:
some eight or nine capitalists in addi
among them old John Wedge, the most
servative man on the street. We shall
him hard to manage, but, if he sees that in
invention which we see, and takes hold o
with us, his name on the board of direct
will give the scheme a standing which cani
be got in any other way."

"Well, what do they expect?" asked Ham
ton.

"As we agreed, I have told them nothing (
what they are to see; they are coming here t
dinner, and expect to see something which wil
be worthy their attention. Now, how is it with
you? Are you sure there will be no hitch?"

"Certain ; have no fear. If they can be astonished, be sure they will be. All my stuff was tested last night, and worked perfectly. But we must remember not to let anyone know where the old man lives."

"I know, I know," said Rehkopf, thoughtfully.

"And don't you think it would be better? He wishes it; we have promised to respect that wish; and, besides, will not the very vagueness and mystery which surrounds him add weight to his invention; a sort of power behind the throne, as it were?"

"You misunderstood me, Al," said Rehkopf; "I have no desire to break my promise. I can even see an advantage in his concealment. But we must remove from the secret in some way everything that savors of scheming or fraud, else our hopes will end in disappointment."

"You can fix it, though," queried Hamilton.

"I hope so, but I am nervous and must have a cool head."

"Well, let's go for a walk and spend the time between this and eight," said Hamilton.

So out they went and strolled along the street; Rehkopf at first absorbed in thought, and gazing on everything with eyes that saw nothing. But they had not gone far before Hamilton's happy, careless spirit, which could not long be restrained, gained the ascendency, and gradually drew the mind of the other away from his cares.

At eight o'clock they were back in the office again, welcoming the first comers.

Soon all the expected guests were on hand and chatting comfortably, trying to get at the secret of their hosts. Many remarks were passed on the curtained recess. What was it hiding; would some destructive engine, some model of a flying machine, some beautiful woman, or what would appear? But their curiosity was restrained as to deeds ; the silence and mystery of that hiding-place remained unbroken.

Soon dinner was laid, and, in discussing the repast, questions gave place to jokes and speeches. Curiosity for a time was at rest.

After the dinner was over and the eatables removed, wine and cigars were brought forward and the servants dismissed.

A tremor of excitement ran through the assembled gentlemen as Hamilton, leaving his

seat, drew near the great unknown, saying:
"Gentlemen, I do not propose to say much.
You all expect to be astonished; I assure you
you will be. What is behind this curtain will
speak for itself. I will show it first and explain
afterwards. Will you arrange your chairs so
as to sit where you can all see into this recess?"

For a moment there was silence, Hamilton
standing, with one hand on the curtain, before
him the guests, their shrewd faces turned to the
point where the wonder was to appear.

Wreaths of smoke unnoticed ascended from
half-parted lips; while, in the background, the
long table stood, rich with glistening glass, tall,
convivial bottles, and varied fruits, lying about
in careless profusion.

Hamilton drew the curtain aside.

CHAPTER VI.

THE DISK UNVEILED. — WHAT THE PRESS AND THE INVENTOR SAID.

BEFORE them, suspended from the ceiling by insulated wires, hung a large, polished disk, which Hamilton explained was "both illuminator, reflector, and resonator combined." Running from the back of this disk, at regular intervals around its edge, were a number of wires. A couple of induction coils and a reinforcing battery completed the apparatus.

After all present had carefully examined the mechanism, and its workings had been explained to their satisfaction, Hamilton said,— "This disk, gentlemen, by the kind permission of the manager of the Theatre Vendome, has been connected with a similar disk so arranged in the theatre that, by the aid of a powerful lens, the entire stage and its settings are focused upon it. Another wire leads to the residence of John

Alder, the discoverer, with whom we will communicate later on. I will first open communication with the theatre, and, after seeing the play and demonstrating the reflecting properties of the disk, will attach the coils and reinforcing batteries, and show you its resonant qualities."

For what followed, the reader is referred to an extract from an article in the MORNING POST of November 20th, which, after describing the incidents above related, contained the following : —

" But how can the revelations which followed be described ? Before the gentlemen present, upon the great, illuminated disk was the stage of the Theatre Vendome. The scene was something inexpressible ; something that seemed obscure, transparent, limpid, and many-hued ; it might be likened to deep water. It seemed black, but when the eye plunged into it, it was surprised at seeing figures floating there in a kind of pale, golden atmosphere, as firmly and sharply outlined on the disk as to the audience in the theatre itself. Exit or entrance, actions, the brilliant costumes, or those of more sombre hue, the sensitive disk was quick to seize, quick

to make apparent.   Simple, ingenious, subtle, it
was a grand and impressive sight.

"The play passing in review was 'Othello, the
Moor of Venice;' the scene, a bedchamber in
the castle, with Desdemona in bed, asleep.
Othello enters, stern, cruel; his face a study of
revenge and grief.   He pauses, looks at his
sleeping wife.   An expression of pitying love
passes over his face as he stoops over and kisses
her, once, twice, thrice.   She wakes; turns
toward him, holding out her hands beseechingly;
half rises, as she begs him to spare her life; then
sinks back, as she sees the jealous passion
shake his very frame.   He stifles her.   In the
agony of his soul he falls upon the floor.

"He rises; opens the door; Emilia enters.
Then follows the accusation — the alarm — the
entrance of Gratiano, Montano, Iago, and others.
The scene which followed beggared description.
Emilia is slain by Iago.   Iago is wounded by
Othello, and, up to the point when Lodovico
commands the officers to bring Othello away,
the tragedy had passed in silent majesty.

"At this point Mr. Hamilton attached the
coils and reinforcing batteries.   If what had

passed before was wonderful, that which now occurred was marvellous. From the now resonant disk came the full, rich tones of Othello's voice: —

> " ' Soft you; a word or two before you go.
> I have done the state some service, and they know 't.
> No more of that.   I pray you, in your letters,
> When you shall these unhappy deeds relate,
> Speak of me as I am; nothing extenuate,
> Nor set down aught in malice; then must you speak
> Of one that loved not wisely but too well.
> Of one not easily jealous, but being wrought,
> Perplexed in the extreme; of one whose hand,
> Like the base Indian, threw a pearl away
> Richer than all his tribe; of one whose subdued eyes,
> Albeit unused to the melting mood,
> Drop tears as·fast as the Arabian trees
> Their medicinal gum.   Set you down this,
> And say that in Aleppo once,
> Where a malignant and a turban'd Turk
> Beat a Venetian and traduced the State,
> I took by the throat the circumcised dog,
> And smote him thus.'

"Then came the fatal dagger-thrust from Othello's own hand, who, falling upon the bed by the side of his murdered wife, murmured in broken sobs, ' I kissed thee ere I killed — thee — no way but this — killing myself — to — die — upon a kiss.'

"A short, sad silence followed, broken at last by Cassio, who, in tones of pity, said, 'This did I fear, but thought he had no weapon; for he was great of heart.'

"The last utterance of Lodovico, 'O Spartan dog,' etc.; the fall of heavy draperies, that obscured the stage; the music from the orchestra; a piercing scream; a startled cry of fire; the rush of hurried feet; the long, dread silence, watching the mysterious disk with painful, anxious hearts; the sudden darkness, as the source of light was cut off; the continued quiet, and moments of suspense, expecting to hear ring out upon the quiet air of night the dread alarm of fire; then the feeling of relief, as moment after moment passed away and quiet reigned supreme, completed a scene that can never be forgotten."

In the HERALD of the same date, the closing paragraph of an article entitled, "The Great Cassani as Othello," read as follows: —

"The closing scenes of this great tragedy were not less terrible than that which followed. Scarcely had the draperies fallen, and the orchestra begun its *postlude*, when a piercing scream and the cry of fire rent the air. At once people rushed pell-mell for the exits; men fought like wild beasts; helpless women were knocked down and trampled upon; pushing, crowding, forcing ahead, a mass of tangled, struggling humanity surged toward the doors — which, fortunately, opened in every direction — into the outer air. A number of ladies were severely injured, but none seriously.

"The cause of the panic is explained in the fact that a lady — highly sensitive and in feeble health — had been so wrought upon by the realistic scenes of the evening, that her nerves gave way under the strain, and, with a loud cry, as the audience were passing out, she fell backward into the arms of her friends. Some foolish individual in the galleries, who did not comprehend the cause of the cry, immediately shouted fire. Happily, however, the admirable construction of the Vendome prevented any serious results."

[FROM THE MORNING CALL.]

"After the sensations of the theatre and a brief interval, Mr. Hamilton turned the switch that placed the disk in connection with the laboratory of John Alder, the inventor. Instant with the closing of the circuit, the disk was illumined with a soft, mysterious light, and the observers found themselves in a room supplied with the usual paraphernalia of an experimentalist. With photographic minuteness, every detail was registered upon the sensitive surface, even to the careworn lines in the face of the alchemist, who stood before a glass jar, in which some mixture boiled and hissed, throwing off vapors which were being collected in a receiver at the top. The expression of eager watchfulness upon the face of John Alder, as the effervescence in the mixture subsided, would have been a study for an artist. He was utterly forgetful of the world; his work absorbed him; and it was only when Mr. Hamilton called, that a sense of his being watched dawned upon him.

" 'Mr. Alder,' said Hamilton, 'as previously arranged, there are with me to-night a number of gentlemen who desire to see you and talk with you concerning your discovery, and to know from you something concerning its possi-

bilities. Though I believe they are already satisfied with what they have seen in connection with
the Theatre Vendome, perhaps it might be as
well for you to tell them something further
about it.'

"'I had forgotten it,' replied Mr. Alder; 'I
have just been preparing some ozone from a
new formula and was not aware of the tell-tale
disk registering my operations. Any information I can give the gentlemen, of course, they
may command.'

"One of the gentlemen present asked, 'Mr.
Alder, I notice the light of your room is unlike
anything I have ever seen before. Is it the
effect upon the disk, or is it the light?'

"'It is the light,' responded Mr. Alder. 'Mr.
Hamilton can describe its peculiarities to you;
but this light, however pleasing and soft it may
be to the eyes, is not permanent. In the disk
before you are the possibilities of all future
lighting. By it, light may be conveyed over a
wire from place to place, however remote. The
source of light at present would have to be the
electric light; but after a time, when stations
communicating with each other are established

all over the world, we shall be enabled to live in an atmosphere of perpetual sunlight ; without its heat, however, for it is a reflected light.'

" 'Can a permanent light be obtained without other expense than that attending the first cost of its introduction ? ' inquired another of our party.

" 'Certainly.   Beyond the establishment of the principal, and accelerating stations, with central offices for general use and their maintenance, there would be no expense ; no machinery, no carbons, no electricians, experts or the thousand and one useless and cumbersome army of attendants necessary to the electric light of to-day. Houses, places of business, theatres, etc., may be connected with each other or with some great central line, and, from over thousands of wires, to the remotest parts of the earth, the scenes, the faces, the music, the language and the light of all the earth will be at our command.   If desired, it is possible with a sensitized paper, placed over the surface of the disk, to receive an imprint of whatever may be exposed to the transmitter ; in proportion as the current is intensified or diminished by the action of light, .

decomposition takes place upon the surface of the paper, and the picture or message is complete ; the surface of the disk is in no way injured, either in its light-giving or its resonant qualities by the process. I will give you an idea of the possibilities of the disk as a light-producer. I have only the incandescent lamps, but they will answer.'

"Mr. Hamilton then placed a ground glass screen before the disk, and informed Mr. Alder that all was in readiness, when a brilliant white light filled the room. Nothing could have been more demonstrative of the capacities of the disk than this last exhibition of its versatile power. It surpassed the expectations of every one, and was pronounced by the capitalists present to be a grand success."

CHAPTER VII.

WHAT THE CAPITALISTS SAID.—PLANS FOR THE
PHOTO-ELECTROPHONE COMPANY PROJECTED.

THE evening papers devoted columns of space
to the invention, for they had had time to work
up the matter thoroughly ; something which the
morning journals had not an opportunity for
doing. The EVENING RECORD, for instance,
came out with a three-column display article,
headed :—

PERPETUAL SUNLIGHT!

DARKNESS FOREVER ROLLED AWAY!

THE POSSIBILITY OF TRANSMITTING LIGHT AND
SOUND OVER THE SAME WIRE ESTABLISHED!

MEN TALK WITH, AND SEE EACH OTHER,
THOUGH SEPARATED BY THOUSANDS
OF MILES!!

In this article, the matter which we have
copied from the POST and the other papers, is

thoroughly investigated, but no less enthu-
siastically put. Then, under the sub-head,
"THE FORMATION OF THE COMPANY," the leading facts in regard to the business transactions
afterwards, were given. It happened in this
wise : —

Mr. Hamilton, after the powers of the invention had been thoroughly tested, turned to his
audience, saying : " Is everything perfectly plain
to you, gentlemen ? Can you not see the close
relation in which this discovery stands to our
every day life ? "

"Why, yes, of course," and like remarks came
from the audience.

"With your permission, then," continued
Hamilton, "I will yield my place to Mr. Rehkopf, who will present the financial side."

Hamilton took a seat, and Rehkopf coming
forward, began : —

"Let us start comfortably, gentlemen ; take
a fresh cigar. But," changing his tone, "probably we are too tired. Had we not better
postpone what remains to be done until to-
morrow ? "

There were cries of " No !" "Go ahead !"

"Let's have it all!" and last, but most important, so Rehkopf thought, old John Wedge remarked, that, as they had begun, it would be just as well to finish then and there; and the old man's eyes twinkled with anticipation.

"We will go on then," said Rehkopf.

"This invention was the property of John Alder, the inventor. It is patented in the United States and the Canadas. Mr. Alder himself is strangely averse to all connection with the world and business. He fears that the excitement would shorten his life; in short, of this invention the world would know nothing, if it had remained for him to push it forward. One-quarter interest has been given to me for placing this invention fairly before the public. Mr. Hamilton has been rewarded with another quarter for having learned the mechanical part, in order to represent Alder in the manufacture of the machines and their practical application. You are here, gentlemen, selected by me as the best men to handle this invention. Mr. Hamilton superintended the construction of the model we have just seen at work. Now, as the matter stands, Messrs. Alder, Hamilton, and myself are

the owners of the invention. But we need
money to put it forward properly ; twenty-five
millions of dollars will be needed ; for this
twenty-five millions Mr. Alder proposes to give
another one-quarter interest. For instance, if
we should start a company with one hundred
million dollars capital, represented by one hundred thousand shares of stock, at one thousand
dollars a share, our interest would cover seventy-
five thousand shares, leaving twenty-five thousand to be disposed of. This, at par, would
furnish the necessary capital. Do you wish to
subscribe for it ?"

There was a moment of silence and much
consultation. Those who remained apart sat
still, staring at their boots or something else
almost as interesting ; or walked up and down
the room in an excited way. Suddenly Bruce
crossed over, from where he had been whisper-
ing with Van Dyke, to Rehkopf, and said : "Van
Dyke and I would like to take the one-quarter
interest, but give us till to-morrow to think it
over."

Rehkopf was not quite satisfied with this, and,
looking about him, saw something in the face of

Mr. Wedge which said plainly he had something
to propose. So he continued : " You have heard
the proposition, gentlemen ; have you anything
to say ? "

Mr. Wedge arose slowly to his feet. He
was quite old and had been sitting the whole
evening. His joints seemed to creak, and
spasms of pain chased across his face as he
finally got into position to speak. His firm,
steady eyes took in the whole company, as he
began quietly.

" Let there be no excitement, gentlemen ;
the invention we are asked to handle is too important for haste. I think I see the application
of it to every-day affairs, and I would like to be
a part owner ; but for that, I must have a chance
for exercising that proportion of power which
belongs to the amount of stock I may hold, in
case the time should ever come when it would
be necessary for me to do so to secure my pecuniary preservation. It is just here : this is a
business transaction. You are all, gentlemen,
friends of mine. I don't wish to be understood
as casting the slightest suspicion of possible
treachery on any one ; there is no need. How

often do we see ruptures and enmities, bringing
ruin in their train, born out of misunderstandings,
and bred because such misunderstandings have
not been foreseen. Now, let us look at the
project before us. We, with the exception of
Messrs. Rehkopf and Hamilton, representing
the public, buy one-quarter interest in a project,
of which the originators hold three-quarters.

"These three men hold a majority of the
stock; there is no probability of a split in their
ranks, should a vote on some question of management be called for; hence, we are utterly in
their power. Now, while I would trust my
fortune to these gentlemen, without security,
and pledge my word for their uprightness, still,
this feeling of dependence breeds distrust. The
result under their proposition would be, that we,
who risk our money in this venture, would have,
practically, no voice as to the way in which that
money should be used. If we subscribe for this
one-quarter interest, theoretically we have
power in the management of the company to the
extent of that quarter interest, but actually we
have none as long as the other three-quarters
remain where they are. Let, therefore, a ma-

jority of the stock, instead of this one-quarter interest, be sold, so that the absolute control shall pass from the hands of these three gentlemen, and I am with you."

"There is something in what you say," said Van Dyke. "Bruce and I were hesitating on that very ground." But they finally came to agreement, Rehkopf and Hamilton agreeing to sell in open market thirty thousand shares of the three-quarter interest, within sixty days of the formation of the company.

This plan would give Rehkopf and Hamilton the control of both elections of the company's officers at the first meeting and the first annual meeting, the latter to take place the first Wednesday of January ensuing, making themselves thereby secure, at least for a year, against any unsatisfactory, stock-jobbing management of the company's affairs.

They then adjourned, to meet next day, when the PHOTO-ELECTROPHONE COMPANY was to be organized and officered.

CHAPTER VIII.

THE PHOTO-ELECTROPHONE COMPANY IS A FACT. —
THE EXPLOSION OF THE PANAMA CANAL. — SEPA-
RATION OF THE CONTINENTS OF NORTH AND
SOUTH AMERICA. — HOW IT WAS SEEN AND HEARD
IN CHICAGO.

NOVEMBER 20th, the Photo-electrophone Company was formed, and officers elected to conduct its affairs until the first annual meeting
that should be held, the first Wednesday of the
ensuing January. Then they immediately began looking about for some means for bringing
the invention more prominently to the attention
of the public.

For months the daily and weekly papers and
monthly magazines had been devoting columns
of their space to the marvels of scientific skill
which were overcoming the barriers in the way
of completing the Panama canal.

A mountain of quartz, that had for years
presented a solid front, defying the puny efforts

of man, was being tunnelled and bored in every direction.

Every appliance that the ingenuity of man could devise was brought to bear upon the diamond-like rock. It was slowly yielding, and what had been abandoned long years ago as impossible of achievement was now looked upon as a matter of time and expense only.

Huge apartments had been hewn out of the solid rock, to serve as magazines, which, in connection with the galleries, were finally filled with an explosive agent, more terrible in its force than either dynamite or nitro-glycerine.

Months of final preparation had been necessary, even after the storing of the explosives. The galleries and air-shafts, for hundreds of feet, had to be filled with cement, which, requiring only a short time to harden, became then as obstinate as the rock itself.

Powerful electric batteries, connected with wires leading to hundreds of explosive points, were stationed some miles distant.

Crowds of the curious, from all parts of the world, were taking up their stations in the mountains around the place, to witness the explosion that was to separate North and South America, and unite the Atlantic with the Pacific Ocean.

Meanwhile, the commercial and scientific world waited. For them a great problem was to be solved. Would the current of the Gulf Stream be changed? Would there be any longer a Gulf Stream? Or, admitting that, would it still continue to flow in the same direction? And would it be with increased or diminished force? were some of the questions discussed by the leading men of the period.

Advanced thinkers were of the opinion that there would be no change — except, perhaps, in the force of the current. The course of the stream, from south to north, was unchangeable, from the very nature of things; for it ran through a valley between submarine mountains, and its course was shaped and controlled by them; that was enough, as far as that was concerned.

The accepted theory of the time was, that the initial force of the Gulf Stream was received through a vast subterranean passage; and it was argued that there could be no greater force exerted through the canal, than through the lower passage. It was stated that an opening as wide and deep as this canal must necessarily be, to be of any service to mankind, would allow such a free course of water as to be unserviceable.

The matter was discussed, pro and con, on all sides, but the projectors of the plans for its completion had said that it must go through, let the cost and result be what it might.

The Photo-electrophone Company, through the efforts of its manager, Mr. Rehkopf, had determined to take advantage of this opportunity, and establish, at any cost, a station upon one of the distant peaks of the Cordilleras, where a powerful lens might hold the hitherto impassable barrier in focus upon a sensitive plate of enormous size ; this, connected by wire with another plate of corresponding dimensions, placed upon the platform of the Temple of Music in Chicago, would give those who could not or did not care to go to the scene itself, an opportunity to witness the explosion, to estimate the effect, as well as to display the powers of their magical disk.

The privilege to use the wire connecting the two disks was generously accorded Mr. Rehkopf by the management of the Inter-Continental Telegraph Company.

All the mechanical details of the plan were left to Hamilton, who reported everything complete a week before the explosion was to take place. The disk had been placed in position, and had responded to all the influences of light upon the transmitter; the whole scene had been reflected upon it, and hundreds of workmen of every nationality were seen engaged in moving machinery and everything else that could possibly be injured by the shock.

Invitations had been sent to the most noted capitalists in the country, who had accepted. In order to satisfy the public interests, since the seating capacity of the Temple was limited, three experts in the art of instantaneous photography, as well as the ablest newspaper men of the day, had been invited.

January 1, the day appointed for the explosion of the obstruction, at last dawned, and the clocks had scarcely indicated nine A.M. when every seat in the vast auditorium was occupied.

Promptly, at half-past nine, Hamilton stepped upon the platform, and, throwing aside the draperies concealing the disk from the audience, revealed a huge, dark-colored, polished mirror, supported in a wooden frame by insulated clamps. A powerful reinforcing battery, a table, upon which were the two points of connection and a Ruhmkorff coil, completed the accessories. Wires from the edge of the disk were gathered at the back to a common centre and joined to the main line of connection.

Instantly, with the closing of the circuit, the audience were introduced to the scene before them by Hamilton, who said, simply : " Morning in the tropics, gentlemen."

A murmur of applause and astonishment ran over the vast assembly as, before them on the face of the disk, they saw a scene familiar to some, but wonderfully real to all. The light greens of the grasses and shrubbery in the uneven foreground, which was broken here and there by rough roadways, piles of timber, workmen's shanties, and great masses of loose rock, contrasted strangely with the darker greens of the cactus and the rich foliage of the Spanish cedar and mahogany on the distant hills; the heads of the feathering palms rising against the deep blue sky ; the long, low line of that portion of the canal already finished ; the barrier with its tints of brown and gray raising its forest-covered crest in the middle distance; while, further away, in fine perspective, the hills glowed and glistened under the angry glare of the equatorial sun, making the scene at once delightful and impressive. No sign of life was there ; absolute silence reigned.

For an hour the audience watched the passive scene on the face of the mirror, without a sign of impatience. Although the picture was becoming familiar, every eye was riveted upon it, watching the shadows come and go in the wonderful play of sunlight.

Precisely at twenty-eight minutes of eleven, a low, rumbling sound from the disk was quickly followed by a dull, heavy roar. The great hill reeled to and fro for a second, when the whole face of the disk seemed covered with masses of flying rocks, trees, and earth ; while from beneath a dull, red glare — as it were from the mouth of hell — threw up angry tongues of flame and smoke. Crash followed crash, as the thousands of tons of rock and earth, hurled heavenward, fell back upon the whirling, rushing waters, that now came tearing through, in the mighty sweep of the Pacific to the Gulf. The air was filled with aqueous vapor, created by the heat and falling masses. It seemed as if the disturbance would never cease; that the effect of the explosion might be calmly and uninterruptedly surveyed.

The rumbling continued to increase; the landscape in the nearer foreground rose and fell, as if disturbed by some greater force than had been reckoned on. Suddenly the waters rose to a terrific height; wave after wave, gathering in force as it increased in volume, rearing its foaming, ragged crest aloft, dashing, breaking, recovering, and breaking again, rolled inland from the Gulf.

Some one in the audience suddenly cried :—
" The Keystone to the arch has fallen out ! South America is no longer a continent, it is an island !"

There could be no dispute about it, startling as it seemed to them. The waters were rising higher and higher, until, with the noise of thunder that through the hall reverberated long and loud, a large portion of the Isthmus disappeared. A section extending from coast to coast, and about two miles from north to south, had literally dropped out of sight ; while from the west came a tidal wave, rolling on at race-horse speed and heralding the force, the power and majesty of the Pacific in its all-engulfing sweep to the Atlantic.

Another wave, but of comparatively diminutive proportions, was hastening from the Gulf to meet its companion from the west. As the two bodies met, a long line of seething, foam-covered water marked the spot : and a sound, like that of escaping steam, came from the disk. A second of struggle, and the mightier power of the Pacific prevailing, rolled its waters on and on toward the Atlantic, till lost to sight. Mass upon mass, hill upon hill disappeared, until the opening appeared to be a number of miles in width. The noise and uproar finally ceased, the tumult of the waters subsided, and the extent of the breach could be plainly estimated.

To the southward, nothing but the newly made cliffs of the highlands and the hills be-

yond could be seen; the higher level of the
Pacific had completely submerged the lowlands.
On the north, the hills ended abruptly, and the
lowlands, as on the south, were completely covered with water. Through this new strait, a
broad current flowed swift and strong.

While the audience were gazing spellbound
at the remarkable effect of the explosion, Pro-
fessor Heintzelman, of B——n University, the
guest of the American Geographical Society,
was asked by Hamilton to address the assembly
on the possible influences this unforeseen sepa-
ration of the Continents of America would
have upon the commerce of the world. An
abstract of his remarks will convey to the reader
some idea of the impression made upon the
audience, who listened with breathless attention.

"If you will permit me, gentlemen," he began, "I may be able to explain somewhat of the
calamity, I may say, which we have just witnessed upon the face of this wonderful disk, the
remarkable powers of which we have nearly lost
sight of in its revelations. For many years, the
popular old-time theory of a passage beneath

the Isthmus of Panama, connecting the Pacific
and Atlantic oceans, through which the current
of the Gulf Stream received its impetus from
the pressure continually exerted by the higher
level of the Pacific, has been frowned upon, and
other theories, more or less worthy of attention,
have obtained a place in the scientific works of
our schools and colleges. If there has ever
been a lingering doubt in the mind of any one
as to which of the theories advanced was cor-
rect, the spectacle we have this day witnessed,
removes it. Nothing is wanting tò prove, that
the passage did exist, and that the narrow neck
of land connecting the northern and southern
continents of America was a great natural
bridge. The archway through which the initial
force of the Gulf Stream was constantly exerted, was large enough to allow of the constant flow of water toward the north, yet small
enough to admit only just so much as might
become heated by the rays of the sun in the
vast basin of the Gulf of Mexico, before being
forced upon its journey and mission toward the
far north.

"By the heat which this stream carried with it,

the temperature along the whole line was raised
to a degree that rendered the climate of the
eastern coast of America, and the whole of
southern Europe, agreeable. Now, however,
all is changed. Gentlemen, I tremble for the
result. Not only will some inhabitable por-
tions of the Windward Islands be submerged
by this rise of oceanic level ; but, in the onward
sweep of this tremendous current, will it not
bring other disasters in its train? Now, there
will be no pause for the tropical sun to exert a
genial influence on the cold waters of the Pacific,
nothing but one great, onward rush of chilling
water. The borders of the Arctic region, which
have been held in check by the warmer current,
will necessarily be enlarged by its withdrawal,
and there can be no possible estimate put upon
the attendant dangers to commerce. Drift ice
will henceforth be a terror to navigation, and
the icy blasts of Arctic winters will very much
lower the present thermal line. The temperature of the eastern and southern coast of North
America, of England, and perhaps of Southern
Europe, will be changed. The vinelands of
France will suffer ; and upon the projectors

of this ill-advised enterprise all blame must be laid. Just what will be the extent of the damage, however, the world can only conjecture and wait for."

Other eminent scientific gentlemen, entertaining similar opinions, expressed themselves ; after which the circuit was broken, the audience scattered, and the successful trial of the disk was over.

Part II.

THE EFFECT.

˙ THE EFFECT.

CHAPTER I.

HOW THE WANT OF A GULF STREAM AFFECTED
THE CLIMATE OF THE WORLD. — THE COMPANY
PROSPERS, AND MOVES INTO A NEW HOME.

IT is now the first of July, a year and a half
since the breaking up of the barrier that stood
in the way of the completion of the Panama
Canal. And here, before we go on with our
story, it may be well to state some of the cli-
matic and other changes, which were caused
by this work. The southeastern coast-line of
North America experienced no noticeable change
in temperature. In the northeastern portion,
familiarly known as New England, the diminu-
tion in warmth was considerable. The last winter had been decidedly colder, and the vast
quantities of ice, which nature, unrestrained
by the warm current of the Gulf Stream, had

stored up there at that time, were now cooling
the atmosphere of the northern countries, and
holding out the promise, that the hot, sweltering
dog-days of August would appear no more.

In Great Britain the change was greater still;
the climate there became colder, and the dismal
fogs, caused by the cold north winds striking
the warm waters of the Gulf Stream, passed
away.

The climate of France was cooled. Sleigh-
bells were heard upon the Boulevards of Paris
in the winter, and the national pride in a tropical vintage was humbled.

Surface navigation, perhaps, suffered the most.
But people soon became accustomed to the
changes, and, though some grumblers, as is
always the case, were found to bemoan the
disappearance of "the good old times," by far
the larger number accepted readily the new
order of things, and, in many cases, found it
decidedly more agreeable.

All this time the Company, although offering
nothing of special interest to the reader, was
making great but expected and agreeable changes
in its affairs. Immediately after the Panama

explosion, the first annual meeting was held, when the officers elected on the formation of the company were continued in office. At the last annual meeting also, six months ago, the same officers were re-elected.

When the Company was formed, Bruce and Van Dyke took ten thousand shares each of the one-quarter interest, and the remaining five thousand was subscribed for by all but one of the guests of Rehkopf and Hamilton on the night of the supper. John Wedge was elected President, Rehkopf became financial, and Hamilton mechanical manager; both offices bearing large salaries, while Van Dyke and Bruce were made treasurer and secretary respectively.

The board of directors consists of seven members of the company, — the five officers already mentioned *ex officiis*, and two other members; these all are holding their positions at the present time.

When, after the first annual meeting, the thirty thousand shares were sold according to agreement, the part which the Photo-electrophone took in showing up the Panama explosion, had created such a boom in the stock, that the shares sold at a large advance over par. This thirty thousand shares was made up of five thousand shares from Alder's one-quarter interest, and the rest divided between Rehkopf and Hamilton; and, when sold, brought snug little fortunes to these three.

The growth of the Company financially was rapid, for its affairs were managed on the most business-like and progressive principles. The Company had hardly been organized before patents were asked for and granted in every country not already covered. In a month's time agents were out showing up the invention, and it was not long before every mail coming in, brought petitions from newly organized companies asking for franchises, giving them the sole right to use the invention in this or that state, county, or city. These franchises were sold for so much cash down, and a percentage of the buyers' profits. Then the Photo-electrophone Company was firmly established on the high road to fortune; while a rapidly increasing surplus, and large and frequent dividends, gratified all concerned.

But the Company made no halt at the sale of

franchises; as it was, the places farthest east
used, by a well-constructed and equitable system
of exchange, the sunlight of those west, as
long as it lasted. One part of the globe, however, proved backward in adopting the invention. There was no company in Asia, and sunlight was not received on any plate there.
Hence, there were about five hours in the night-
time when the supply of sunlight failed ; then
recourse was had, by the various companies, to
the improved electric light. To get over this
difficulty, the parent Company was now on the
point of establishing stations in Asia, solely for
the reception of light which they expected to
transmit and sell to the various sub-companies.

The Company has just established its head-
quarters on its own ground ; having moved two
months ago into a new building which it built
and specially adapted for its own use, at the
corner of Grand Street and Loan Avenue. The
ground floor, thrown into one large room, is
devoted to business ; and fifty clerks, more or
less, each with territorial divisions under his
special charge, keep guard of the interests of
the Company there.

The floor above is devoted to the use of Rehkopf's department. In the front is the manager's private room, while the rest of the floor is divided up into little rooms, where more clerks, two or three in a room, attend to the correspondence.

On the third floor, at the back, is a large hall for stockholders' meetings. In the front room the board of directors hold their meetings, and this is fitted up with exquisite luxury in every way ; comfortable and substantial furniture, thick rugs, rich hangings, and pictures of the greatest artistic merit.

Lastly, on the top floor, is Hamilton's department, the private office and laboratory in front, and the remaining space thrown into one large workshop for construction and experiment.

The appointments of the building are first-class in every respect. Three large elevators, one for private use, one for the public, and one for merchandise, are in constant motion, up or down. Every room is connected with every other by the magical disk.

Rehkopf's, Hamilton's, and the board of directors' rooms, are all connected with Mr.

Alder's laboratory ; thus Mr. Alder can be present at the board meetings without bringing himself into contact with men, and, if need be, give
advice to the directors, to Rehkopf, or to Hamilton, without delay.

Such is the state of the Company and its
affairs. Naturally, we look for new developments in the affairs of Alder, Rehkopf, and
Hamilton, because it must be remembered they,
on the sale of their stock a year and a half ago,
found themselves in the sudden possession of
what would have seemed boundless wealth to
them six months before that time. Although
it is a 'fact that the sudden acquisition of wealth
has a tendency to change a person and his plans,
especially if that person's character be not positive and settled, still, in the case of Alder and
Rehkopf, it made no change, for they were men
of settled character ; and money, while it gave
them a better condition of life, changed in no
way their life's motives. Alder, his wealth in-
vested in safe ways under Rehkopf's advice, is
to be found working out new plans in the same
old place, far removed from the world and
undisturbed by men and their affairs. Mankind

knows of him, but does not know him. What surplus of money he has he devotes in a quiet way towards helping forward deserving students throughout the country.

Rehkopf is the same practical business man of few words. Though not sparing of money in his way of life and in the entertainment of his friends, still, naturally, he throws none away. When we first knew him he was inclined to speculation, because he was then poor and wanted wealth; now, in the enjoyment of good fortune, he has lost the desire for taking risks, and invests his money for security only. As he finds it impossible to spend his income, his wealth rapidly and silently increases, while he throws into the Company's interest his whole time and skill.

We turn to Hamilton as the one most liable to show the effects of a change in fortune, because he was always unsettled in character and careless of money. Hamilton has grown luxurious. His bachelor quarters are renowned for their magnificence all over the city. His servants are many in number and the best paid; his pictures are the finest money can buy; the horse he rides is the most valuable one in the country. He always finds some money to put into the pet schemes of his friends, and as he never takes the trouble to investigate, such investments, in nine cases out of ten, turn out ruinous. Even with this drain on his purse, however, his income is all-sufficient. The fortune realized on the sale of the stock is, owing to Rehkopf's persistency, well placed and still intact. Beyond all this, he has found his sphere, and his occupation acts upon him like a balance wheel. His position in the Company is one of great responsibility ; consequently, of honor. It absorbs his time, furnishing him day by day with new ideas, in the development and application of which, for the good of the Company, he loses himself.

CHAPTER II.

INTRODUCES NEW AND IMPORTANT ACTORS.

WE have seen how, from the meeting of
Hamilton and Rehkopf, the invention of John
Alder came to be placed on the market ; how it
became appreciated and popular; how it drew
capital about it and repaid the same many times;
how it stands now a grand mechanical and financial success. We have noted also, though briefly,
what changes, if any, this success has wrought in
the characters of the three originators. It now
remains to show the results of this success and
the changes on the lives and futures of these
men: a task difficult and complicated, since
new and important actors have stepped upon
the scene. These are William Van Rense and
his family.

Several months ago the name William Van.
Rense appeared on the books of the Company
as the holder of a few shares of stock. Since

that time he has increased his interest largely. Immediately on his first connection with the Company, he appeared in person at the office, asking leave to seé some of the most important features of the invention. On that and succeeding visits he made the acquaintance, and in most cases the friendship, of the directors. In return for their kindness he invited them to his home, a house which he had bought and fitted up in a sumptuous manner, in a most fashionable part of the city.

In connection with other business, he made himself felt among the financiers on the street, acquiring their respect and esteem; and it was not long before he came to be looked upon as an authority, and his opinions were quoted everywhere. The directors, therefore, while partaking of his hospitality, found many topics for conversation of mutual financial interest, and Mr. Van Rense soon came to be regarded as decidedly a useful member of the Company.

To the curious he is continually an interesting object for study. Of his history as a man nothing is known. He speaks many foreign languages fluently, but he is considered an American by those who have observed his mode of thought and the ease with which he assumes the peculiarities of our institutions.

Personally he is tall, well made, with iron gray hair and dark eyes. A mustache partially conceals his firm-set, resolute mouth; all the rest of his face is clean-shaven. He would be a remarkable man to any one, and his peculiar reticence and unknown history render him doubly so.

Mrs. Van Rense is of medium height, fair, and with large blue eyes. In her face there still linger many traces of youthful beauty, but the lines have been subdued and softened with time ; and, while there is an air of·sadness about her, the result, perhaps, of a peculiar temperament, or of some secret sorrow, her family relations are of the pleasantest; herself and husband a unit, each studying the happiness of the other, and the attention on the part of the husband is most considerate at all times. The devotion of both is strong, lasting, not put forward for show.

Mrs. Van Rense never has anything to say of herself to her acquaintances, jealously guards every avenue of approach to her past, considers the comfort of her friends with evident solicitude, and is happy in anticipating every little unnoticeable, unexpressed wish of her husband.

The only other member of the family is a daughter Laura, a beautiful maiden of perhaps twenty-one years, fair, with blue eyes, and with rippling golden hair. She was either born in Europe, or, leaving this country when very young, has been schooled by her father and mother into forgetfulness of it. Certainly she never says anything that would give any one a clew to their early history.

Such is the family that is now rapidly eating its way into the heart of the aristocracy by sheer force of wealth and evident breeding, while everything concerning its origin is pure conjecture.

With such a man as Van Rense interested in the Company, and taking an active part in finance, it was not strange that he, on the death of one of the directors, should be looked upon as a valuable man for the place. He was approached on the subject, and signified his will-

ingness to accept the position ; so, on the 2d
of July, being the first Wednesday of the
month, and, according to by-laws, the regular
day for the semi-annual meeting, he was elected
a director.

CHAPTER III.

EVENING AT CLIFFS, IN WHICH ALDER'S OLD ENEMY
IS DISCLOSED AT HIS ELBOW, AND THE CHAP-
TER, THOUGH ONE OF LOVE AND ROMANCE, HAS
A TRAGIC INTEREST.

THEY were sitting this evening together,
Mabel and her father, in a sort of observatory
on the edge of the cliffs,— that bold, high
promontory, which, rising perpendicularly from
the waters of the lake to a towering height,
gives to Alder's home its name. The place
which they occupied was the broad, level surface of a rock rising above the plateau where
the house was built, and commanding, backward, a view of the road, which descended,
steep and straight, for some distance, until lost
in the woods. In front, from beneath their feet,
stretching far away, spread the lake, dark and
cold, reflecting the rich, warm light from cottage windows and the steely glitter of the stars.

Lately, — that is, since the coming of warm weather, — it had been the custom of Mabel and her father to devote this part of the day to a *siesta*, at which Hamilton was frequently present; the latter, while studying the invention under Alder, previous to the formation of the Company, had, as already hinted, found some thing agreeable in the society of Mabel, and was now in the habit of spending his leisure hours with her. They were both young, congenial, and appreciative of each other; what wonder was it, therefore, that Hamilton, finding himself rich on the success of the Company, and all barriers to the establishment of a suitable home for himself removed, should take away from his actions that restraint which a man feels who cannot fulfil an implied promise.

Then, too, a new factor had made its appearance in Mabel's character; Love had come; she felt his breath, and, though her youth had been passed amid the dust and mould of science, she responded to the touch of the god perhaps more readily than one would who had been brought up in a more congenial atmosphere. Too unaccustomed to the world to dissemble her feelings, she yielded easily to Hamilton's influence, and they drifted into that close relationship to each other, which only requires some little, unexpected circumstance to bring to a matrimonial crisis.

Now it was almost night; she was waiting for Hamilton's coming. He had not put in an appearance for a week, —.an unexpected, and to her unexplainable, break in his visits; these visits had been a part of her very existence, and, missing them, she felt lonely and disturbed. Time passed unconsciously except in the aggregate; seconds and minutes were unnoticed, but the hours lagged by with leaden feet. In the twilight, just now, she had been watching the children at play on the shore of the lake, and the laughing, rollicking rowing parties. Night dropped, with the dew, romance into the valley, while the atmosphere of the Cliffs seemed heavy with melancholy as she sat there motionless, absorbed in thought and waiting.

Mr. Alder, always trying something new, had arranged a hand-reflecting disk, and was testing it this evening. The light was brought to this plate over wires from an electric light in his studio; and he sat lazily turning it, and studying the effect of the shaft of light that shot from it. But Mabel was out of tune for such experiments. She had been silent for a long time, apparently listening, when suddenly, in a low, excited tone she asked, "Don't you hear a horse, father?" Then, without waiting for an answer, "It must be Albin; he has n't been here for a week."

Then Alder turned the hand holding the disk, and a beam of dazzling light flashed down the road. The noise of hoofs became more distinct, and finally, at the far end of the road, the well-known horse and rider dashed out from under the trees. They saw him pull up when he found the fiercely-blazing dragon's-eye of light upon him; but he came on again.

Mabel, knowing well where he would tie his horse, hastened there before him. They had not met for over a week, and this delay had stored up in their minds feelings they had not known before. They said nothing, but their silence was eloquent; their hand-clasps were more warm and lingering; they felt utterly at home and at peace with each other, until Hamilton's question, "Where is your father?" with its freedom from sentiment, broke the silence, and startled them both.

"Father is on the rock; do you wish to see him very much?" with a sigh.

"Well, yes; I wished to give him the results of an election, and some minor details of the Company."

They went direct to the rock. There they found the old man, careless of everything but the power of his little ray of light, which continued to dart here and there over the valley and lake in front and below him.

"You seem to have lost all interest in the Company," said Hamilton, after the compliments of the evening had been passed; "nothing has been heard from you for some time. However, everything is satisfactory, I think; no change, except in the election of a new director."

"Then there was no need of me," said Alder. "Besides, I have been very busy." But he did not say what the business was, although he ended the sentence with an inflection that

promised something more, and there came a
silence. The old man's hand opened and shut,
as though in imagination he already had a grip
on the subject of his investigations, as he fell
back into a reflective mood. The ray of light
danced unheeded across the country; but finally,
an idea dawning upon him that he had not
ended his sentence with a vocal period, he
repeated, "very busy," dropping his voice, and
the silence became deader than ever.

"Well, I don't know that there was any actual
need of your attention," said Hamilton. "It
seems to me as if everything is satisfactory."

The conversation then drifted off from one
subject to another for some time, until another
long pause brought attention back to the original theme.

"By the way," said Hamilton, "I have n't
told you anything of our new director; he is
comparatively a stranger among us, but a man
who promises to be of more than ordinary service to the board."

"So?" said Alder, inquiringly, yet as one
who was not anxious to have his question answered.

"Yes, but he is a peculiar man. No one seems to know anything about him, except that he is respected in business circles, has plenty of money, and that his name is William Van Rense."

The ray of light that had been wandering across the country, became suddenly fixed in place, and seemed to burn with a fiercer glow as it fell on the sombre house that stands in the valley beside the road. This name, so innocent to others, fell upon John Alder's ear with a fearful shock. His air-castles vanished at the sound of it, and he saw arise before him the ghost of his miserable past. With it all a sickening dread overpowered him, the fear that this was but the first ripple of a returning tide of worldly cares, disappointments, and misfortunes, which he had thought never would rise again. Like all men of intelligent minds, he was easily impressed. One stroke of adversity, coming at a time of supreme peace, took instant hold of him, and more strongly because of the contrast.

If Mabel had had eyes for what was passing; if she had ever heard that name before; if her father had appeared different from ordinary, her attention would have been attracted to him, and she would have seen the gray head sink lower and lower, till the face was almost hidden in the long, white beard.

But in a moment Alder arose and slowly, with bowed head, descended the steps, crossed the plateau, and entered the house. In his hands, which were clasped behind him, he held the disk with a care, the result of training, not of any effort of the mind, the wire trailing behind him on the ground. The beam of light danced in grotesque curves and mocking motions, now over fields and woods, now off into space, as though seeking the farthest stars.

He passed from sight without a word, but that was nothing remarkable in itself with those who were well acquainted with him; his departure left Hamilton and Mabel together.

"Did you notice how the light lit up that queer, big house down in the valley?" said Mabel.

"Yes, I was thinking of that, and how all such houses seem to have secrets to tell." While speaking, he moved his seat to one by the

side of his companion, and took one of her
hands in the darkness; that hand was not with-
drawn, but everything seemed listening all at
once; and, let him sink his voice to a whisper,
the words seemed to clash in his ears. "I
wonder, Mabel, if there is any house anywhere,
sombre or gay, that could tell me the secret of
our future; — will you be my wife?"

The hand in his grasp trembled a little, but
soon the other came to join it; softly pressed
his hand between them, lifted it and laid it over
her heart. They joined their hearts there in the
soft evening air, as they had joined their hands,
not with hesitation, wavering, and excitement,
as people who enter a new relationship, but in
quietness and peace, as one who takes but
another step along a pleasant path, whose end
has been seen from the beginning.

For a long while they sat there together;
from the water came now and then a faint ripple of laughter, or a bit of song; from the land
the busy cricket's cry. One by one the farmhouse lights went out, the voices from the lake
were hushed, yet these two kept their places,
talking low, until the big moon rose over the

distant hills. It was far into the night, but that was nothing at the Cliffs.

At last, Hamilton, arousing himself to action, said, "I will ask your father's consent without delay. He is at work in his laboratory, for I see the light there; let 's go to him now."

At the laboratory door they separated; Hamilton entered and Mabel passed on.

CHAPTER IV.

HAMILTON'S PROPOSITION TO ALDER, AND HOW IT WAS ANSWERED.

As Hamilton entered the room, John Alder was standing at the farther end before a curiously contrived box, which was connected by rubber pipes with a number of hermetically-sealed receivers, and also with an air pump which the alchemist was then operating.

Absorbed in his experiment, Alder paid no attention to the entrance of Hamilton, who was also too much interested in his own mission to notice, at all accurately, any of the details of the work before the experimentalist. Nay, even, Hamilton had already commenced the story of his love for Mabel, and had begun to call attention to his present prosperous condition and his ability to take a wife, before Alder indicated that he was aware of the presence of any one else in the room.

"Eh?" said Mr. Alder, turning suddenly and facing Hamilton.

"I was saying," continued the latter, "that if there ever was a time when I was prepared to take a wife, to support and indulge her in all that she could wish for, since the golden flood of prosperity has rolled away all possibilities of doubt as to my future, that time is now. I have talked with Mabel, and we await your consent to our union. I think I can promise you, in myself, a dutiful son. She will not be separated from you, and " —

"I know of no reason," interrupted Alder, "why you should not marry whenever it suits you, Hamilton. I had hoped that I should not lose my daughter quite so soon ; but it is proper, proper ; — I don't know of anything more I can say. I am interested in a new experiment, which is absorbing my attention — just now ; — like to have you look at it some timè, not to-night — not to-night ; — to-night will show whether my calculations have been right or wrong," muttered the old man as he left Hamilton to himself, to go or stay as he pleased.

CHAPTER V.

HAMILTON IN HIS ROOM PONDERS OVER THE SITU-
ATION, AND IS INTERRUPTED BY ALDER, WHO
SHOWS SOMETHING STARTLING ON THE FACE OF
THE DISK.—A KNOCK AT THE DOOR.

HAMILTON, two weeks after was sitting in his
room in the Company's building, late one afternoon. A meeting of the board had been held
that day which, after a short session, was adjourned a half hour ago. There was nothing of
special interest in the meeting, however, and
Hamilton, leaving the other members to their
talk and cigars, sought his own room. Do what
he would, the lines of his life seemed somewhat
mixed, and there appeared to be motives in the
lives of his friends for which he could find no
explanation or warrant.

In the first place, he has just left a man, William Van Rense, downstairs, who is a decided
mystery to him. Van Rense is so quick to see
an advantage, and so ready to show the way for

turning that advantage to account in the business affairs of the Company, that he has made
himself a most important factor in its management.   Still there is no known point in his past
from which a reliable estimate of his future
operations could be deduced.   That he had
great business qualifications, every one knew;
but otherwise he was shrouded in mystery, and
mystery is productive of distrust.

Hamilton, from the sensitiveness of his character, was especially open to such influences,
and, from the prominence of this person in his
own circle, his secret was a vexatious subject of
thought.

His relations with Mabel, growing pleasanter
day by day, were a bright spot in his life.   In
her companionship he forgot his cares, and,
when away from her and regarding her more
objectively, other people came into his thoughts
in connection with her, — her father, for in
stance.

As soon as Hamilton came to consider Mr.
Alder and his actions, just then he entered
mazes of thought which seemed unsolvable.
Two events, of late occurrence, clung to his

mind with an incredible persistency, compared
with the want of effect these same events had
on other people. To begin at the beginning, he
was disturbed at the manner of Mr. Alder, when,
two weeks ago, he met him in the laboratory
and asked for Mabel's hand. His thoughts, in
this regard, assumed a more important and
absorbing interest the more he put his wounded
self-love out of the question, and tried to look at
the interview with the old man in an unpreju-
diced light.

He tried to remember what Alder was doing,
when he entered the laboratory ; but could not
recall anything but the vaguest outlines, though
he hunted in all the old man's actions for some
clew to the case ; and, as end and total, there remained nothing but the disturbing remembrance
of Alder, wild-eyed and nervous, highly excited
but apparently absorbed in his work, treating
his daughter's marriage as a thing of no moment,
something over which he was not willing to
spend an instant of serious thought.

Then, too, Alder had kept himself invisible
ever since that night, although Hamilton had
found his way to the Cliffs every evening.

Mabel had said that her father was "very busy, and wished to stay by himself," and did not seem to be in the least disturbed.

But Hamilton, although he tried to regard it in the light of an usual occurrence, could not help but feel that there were strange, hitherto unnoticed peculiarities in Alder's actions lately. He found himself, as a consequence, unable to throw off a feeling of nervousness and foreboding for the future. In this state of mind he was sitting in his room that afternoon, when the voice of Mr. Alder, speaking through the Photo-electrophone, startled all his meditations into flight.

"I have got something to show you," said the voice.

"What's up?" thought Hamilton, as he cut off the light from his room, in order to make the representations on the disk more distinct, mentally recording, at the same time, the fact that Alder's voice seemed full of excitement.

As the room was darkened, on the face of the disk appeared the well-known laboratory of John Alder. Hamilton instantly recognized an apparatus similar to, but on a more extensive

scale than, the one he had seen in the laboratory on the night of his proposal to Mabel. A
long, coffin-shaped box, with a glass side, showing the inanimate form of a boy, rested upon a
table in the middle of the room. As before, a
number of glass jars and an air-pump were connected with the box by heavy rubber tubes;
check-valves were arranged, so as to prevent
any back pressure upon the jars. An indicator
on the top of the box, something like a steam
gauge, showed the pressure to be fifteen pounds
to the square inch.

"Is this your new experiment?" queried
Hamilton.

"Ah, yes," said Alder, looking up from the
box, and toward the disk. "I have made a
discovery which is more wonderful in its results
than anything which has ever before been developed."

"What is the nature of it?" asked Hamilton.

"The preservation of the human body, so
that it is practically proof against disease and
death."

"A consummation devoutly to be wished
for," muttered Hamilton.

Then Alder, elevating his voice, — something unusual with him, even when greatly excited, — began a description of his discovery, and its methods of operation, hurrying along with scarcely time for breath between the sentences, and allowing no opportunity for interruption. It ran as follows : —

"Some time ago I discovered that, by submitting the flesh of animals to a certain process, it was possible to preserve them without the aid of either salt or sugar; that certain gases could be generated, possessing the same antiseptic qualities as these two articles, but, unlike them, imparting no taste or odor to the food preserved.

"After experimenting in this direction for years, I discovered combinations of different salts, which can be easily converted into gases without losing any of their antiseptic qualities, and will preserve all kinds of food for almost any length of time. But, for the most part, these preparations are useless, as they render the food unfit for use; not because of any unpleasant taste imparted, but from the fact that, while depriving the food of the elements of destruction, the elements necessary to digestion are also taken away.

" In conducting a series of experiments with chlorine, phosphorus, and ozone, I hit upon a process, by which it was possible to preserve beef, fish, and vegetables for an indefinite period without the aid of any other agent; and that, while the elements of destruction were forced out or neutralized, the preserving element was absorbed, and the material so processed would not only be imperishable, but, acted on by the juices of the stomach, became more easily and naturally digested than in its original state. My ozone I prepare so that it is like a modification of oxygen produced by a succession of electric sparks, by which it is made to assume a more active condition; the ozone is then phosphorized and the three elements brought together and applied in the ordinary way.

" It occurred to me some time ago that, by altering the methods of application somewhat, it might be possible to treat a live animal to this process, the elements of death neutralized and the requisites of life absorbed in their stead; that the animals so treated would, in consequence of the decreased waste, live for a period only limited by the inhalation of the poisonous gases from the atmosphere, which would affect the tissues in time to such an extent, that it would be necessary to renew the process in order to lengthen out the life. The food eaten would all be processed, and there would be nothing to prevent the life of an animal from being extended fifty or seventy-five years by a single process, which could be renewed whenever that seemed to have lost its power.

"I experimented with a number of small animals, rabbits, dogs, and such like, before I succeeded in mixing the gases properly; my greatest difficulty being to prevent the liquefying of the gases under the slight pressure I was compelled to submit them to. I succeeded at last in getting my theories down to the proper mixing proportions, and treated a rabbit to the process, which passed through successfully. To be sure, this was only week before last, but the gases used in this case were the same as those used by me in preserving a hind-quarter of lamb over a year ago, and the meat is, to-day, as sweet and fresh as ever.

"The rabbit passed through the process successfully, and is now more lively than usual. He eats and drinks little or nothing, and then only such food and water as have been processed for it. I have experimented with a number of animals since, every one coming out safely and with renewed vigor. On depriving some of these animals of life, and examining their flesh, I have found no difference in its quality from that which had been processed after being slaughtered.

"In this connection I have long thought it possible to utilize this discovery for the benefit of mankind; believing that, if it was possible to preserve the body of a living animal so as to render it comparatively imperishable, it was possible to apply the same treatment to a living human body, thereby arresting decay and extending indefinitely the lease of life. I became satisfied that it could be done without danger or without any particular inconvenience, the only thing necessary being to produce temporarily suspended animation.

"In looking around for a subject I came upon this boy. He is the son of a neighbor; his parents, without knowing precisely what was wanted, consented to his assistance in some experiments I was about to make. The parents are both scrofulously inclined; all their other seven children are long since dead of consumption; this boy himself has been afflicted for some time with a cough and other symptoms, indicating that he too was passing slowly into a decline. Promising to save his life, I obtained his consent to treatment. I then produced suspended animation by means of hypodermically injecting a solution — the composition of which I shall never reveal — placed him in this box, sealed it hermetically, and, by the use of this pump, I exhausted the air, and, at the same time, forced in the compound gases before alluded to. The pressure on the body is at all times fifteen pounds to the square inch. After the body has remained under the influence of these gases three hours, it should be removed and submitted to a current of electricity, when respiration will be restored and the operation be complete.

"This boy," continued Alder, without rest, and pointing to the body before him, " has been under the influence of the gases the required time; I will now remove him, and restore him to consciousness."

Saying which, John Alder, with trembling hands, opened the valves communicating with the atmosphere, took away the front of the box, drew the body of the boy out upon the metallic slab, and was just applying a current of electricity, when some one knocked at the door of Hamilton's room.

"Come in," cried Hamilton, never taking his eyes from the face of the disk.

CHAPTER VI.

IN WHICH VAN RENSE GROWS THOUGHTFUL AT
THE SIGHT OF A FACE, AND PUTS QUESTIONS
TO WHICH HE GETS UNSATISFACTORY ANSWERS.

VAN RENSE entered, for it was he who
knocked at the door. He did not disturb the
communication that was going on between
Hamilton and Alder; the former was too much
absorbed in what he was looking at. Van Rense
found himself immediately interested in the
actions of Alder, as shown on the plate, and,
at the same time, at liberty to devote his whole
attention to them. Coming, as he did, when the
causes which led up to the present effect had
been explained and the hoped-for result already
hinted at, he had lost all information as to what
had gone before, or what was to come after, and
saw but the present state of the case. His face
betrayed no sign of what was passing in his
mind, but it would not be unnatural to suppose

him imagining himself present at some blas-
phemous attempt at resurrection, when he saw
the seeming corpse of the boy stretched out stiff
and motionless under the hand of the chemist.
Slowly his eye wandered from the pallid face
to Alder's haggard countenance, covered with
beard. Something in it caught his attention,
for his gaze became fixed and intense, never to
wander from it back to the events going on.
Indeed, his own face, now, for the first time,
proved treacherous, and could any one have
watched it at that moment, in the disturbed
features he would have seen the shadow of some
great event in his life.

Slowly and noiselessly he stepped backward
to the door, opened it and left; passed along
the hall in deep thought, his head bowed, his
face locked in the same fixed expression, and
his hands clasped behind his back. On he
went, regardless of the elevator which had
brought him up and was now waiting for him,
down the stairs slowly, step by step.

The door of the board-room was open as he
came to it, and old John Wedge was sitting in
full view, reading a paper in the window. An

idea came to Van Rense. He stopped, threw out from his face all traces of disturbance, entered the room, and as he sauntered carelessly up to Mr. Wedge, said, "Well, the whole machine seems to be in the stocks. I'm just back from a walk through the building and saw no signs of life anywhere."

"Yes," replied Wedge, "the business department is the only one doing any work at present; there is hardly any need of a board of directors, the system of the Company is so good."

"No need of work from them, at least, though, I suppose, when the reservoirs of light in Asia are finished, complications will arise that may make our brains useful."

"By the way, where's Rehkopf?" asked Wedge; "he was not at the board meeting to-day."

"He is out riding with my daughter. Hamilton, though, is upstairs. I dropped into his room just now, but saw that he was deeply interested in something reproduced by the electroscope, so I left."

"Did you notice what it was?"

"Not particularly," replied Van Rense. "A

tall man, with gray whiskers, seemed to be trying some experiment."

"That was Alder himself, probably, showing
up something new. He is always working at
something, — greatest genius the world ever
knew."

"So that's Alder. I never saw him before;
have been, hitherto, too deeply interested in the
invention to care about the inventor. Now,
after seeing him, I think I should like to know
him," said Van Rense, hesitatingly, like one who
is but repeating, in a fit of abstraction, a lesson
already learned.

"Well, you will find that a difficult job. In
the first place, on the formation of the Company, John Alder stipulated that no one should
bother him with its affairs, and to make this
more sure, he never permitted any one to see him
in his home, from the fact that no one, do what
he may, has been able to find out where it is,
except Hamilton and Rehkopf; those two knew
Alder before the Company was formed; in
fact, they formed the Company, and have, owing
to promises to Alder, as they say, kept his home
a secret. Some of the stockholders once,

thinking they would like to unearth him, tried
to follow out the wires leading to his house, but
these wires were connected with those leading
to the old office, where the Company was called
into existence, and hence they were thrown off
the track there, for the direction of the old lines
is unknown to every one but Hamilton, who
superintended the laying of them. For all you
and I know, or will know, he may live in the
moon. It is strange that he wants to keep himself so close."

"And stranger still that he manages to," said
Van Rense, carrying out the thought. "I
should think you might draw him out while
talking business."

"That's of no use," said the other; "when he
has said his say about the affairs of the Company, he remarks that he is busy, and you find
the circuit is suddenly broken."

"Doesn't Hamilton visit him often?"

"Yes, every day or two, I believe, and, from
the fact that he spends so much time here, you
might conclude that he had not far to go; but
modern motion is almost as quick as thought,
and all that sort of thing, you know; at any

rate, if you want to find him you must make up your mind to look over a circle whose radius is about two hundred miles. It strikes me that, in the face of such odds, the chances of success are rather slim."

"What of his family; what has become of his wife?" inquired Van Rense.

"I never heard that word mentioned in connection with him. But what's the use; there's little satisfaction to be got out of me or any one else save Rehkopf and Hamilton, and they are dumb on that subject," said Wedge, taking up his paper again.

After a few questions and answers concerning the affairs of the Company, Van Rense relapsed into deep thought, and, clasping his hands as before behind his back, departed homeward, muttering, while descending the steps, or among the crowds on the thoroughfares, or in the shadow of his own doorway, "Not dead! not dead!" like the vocal echo of a conviction that had fallen on his mind with the weight of a millstone.

CHAPTER VII.

WHEREIN HAMILTON MEDITATES ON THE POSSI- .
BILITIES OF ALDER'S DISCOVERY, AND HOW HE
EXPLAINS IT TO THE DIRECTORS.

AFTER the interview with John Alder had
been brought to a sudden termination by the
breaking of the circuit at the laboratory, Hamilton sat back in his chair, and pondered over
the discovery just revealed to him.

"Was it all that it claimed to be? If so, it
was of the greatest importance to humanity;
with the means and absolute control of the
forces at hand, that would put to flight the King
of terrors, there would be no limit unattain-
able by man. No longer would the first half of
life be spent in getting ready to live the second
half; no longer years of regret over opportunities wasted and hopes deferred; no longer the
necessity of crowding into the narrow limits of
threescore years and ten the preparations, trials,

cares, joys, sorrows, and failures so common to the large majority of humanity. On the other hand, with the certainty of continued life, barring accidents, there would be plenty of time for every one to follow out the bent of his own inclination, and nothing would stand in the way of the absolute, ultimate success of all. A new race of beings would spring into existence, with more intelligence, more ability, a wider range of experience and comprehensive knowledge, fitted for any field of action. John Alder had been too close a student in the past, too accurate an observer of the laws of cause and effect, to be misled by any half-developed theory. His photo-electrophone, the present method of illumination and intercommunication, is a marvel of scientific accomplishment. I have seen with my own eyes things I could hardly bring my mind to believe, and have more than once been astounded ; to be sure, this is of vastly more importance than anything which has preceded it, but so have been all the other discoveries. But what has come over Alder lately ? What makes him seem so strange ? I wonder if there is anything the matter with him, or if the fault is all with me ! Anyway, I will take this matter to Wedge, and see what he thinks of it ; " and leaving his laboratory, he hastened to the board-room, where he found the president still reading the paper.

Wedge noticed the excitement in Hamilton's face as he came in, and accosted him with :—

"Anything new, Hamilton ? "

"Yes," exclaimed Hamilton ; "I have just witnessed a wonderful scene on the disk in my room. In answer to a call from Alder, I put my plate in connection with his, and witnessed the closing scenes of a process that well nigh robbed me of my senses."

"What is it, another discovery ?" asked two other directors, in a breath, who, coming in just then, added themselves to the group.

"Yes," answered Hamilton.

He then explained, hurriedly, the details of John Alder's discovery, as we have already seen, and, without interruption, continued :—

"The boy had been under the influence of the gases used in the process for about three hours. He was then taken out of the box, and placed on a metallic slab by Mr. Alder. Naked,

and to all appearances pulseless, the boy lay
there as inanimate as a corpse. The poles of a
number of batteries were brought into contact
with the extremities of the body, the current
was applied, and instantly a shudder ran through
his frame. The eyes opened, the chest rose
and fell, and, in another instant, the boy sat up.
The electric current was then shut off, and,
after a thorough rubbing, the boy dressed and
took a seat facing me; there was a healthy
glow in his face, his eyes were bright and
sparkling, and he sat upright, apparently as well
and strong as a young man ever could be. In
obedience to the request of Mr. Alder I questioned him, and, answering, the boy said that
he had never felt so well before; that he had
no pain, no inclination to cough whatever, and
that he felt as if he could jump and run all day
and not be tired."

"What did you say then?" asked Wedge,
who, listening attentively, had not uttered a
word up to this time.

"What could I say?" responded Hamilton.
"I sat like one in a dream, wondering if such
things could be; if the cloud that had hitherto

hung between us and the secrets of perpetual life, had at last been rolled away ; whether it was now in our power to .indefinitely prolong our lives. But there was the boy; his statements concerning his past ; my own observations of his condition previous to restoration ; his statements, and my observation since the treatment. By the development of a process like this, man would not grow old, would be able to maintain always the physical condition of a vigorous, healthy manhood."

" If this thing is a fact," said Mr. Wedge, in a tone of voice that showed his faith in John Alder was not shaken, " I see no reason why we should not utilize it for the benefit of mankind. If it is an established fact, I say ; if, in the excitement of the inventor or discoverer, nothing has been overlooked, no mistakes made, it will be necessary to organize another company to handle it, because the matter is of such vital importance to humanity, that it would be impossible for a company handling it to pay attention to anything else. Let us not be in a hurry, however, gentlemen ; let us wait for a month or two, while Mr. Hamilton keeps track of the boy. If the people in the vicinity of this boy's home; if his father and mother and the boy himself all testify to a continuance of his changed and improved condition, then there will be time enough for us to place it before the public, and begin at once to renew the youth and health of the world."

It was agreed, therefore, that Hamilton should keep watch of the boy, and communicate the ideas of the president and directors to Mr. Alder for his approval; meanwhile the others would await developments.

CHAPTER VIII.

THE SKELETON IN THE VAN RENSE CLOSET. — THEY DETERMINE TO SEEK SOLITUDE.

VAN RENSE walked into the house; once inside, he sought his wife's sitting-room. He found her there and alone.

"Where is Laura?" said he, walking slowly to the window, and, standing there, gazed moodily up and down the street.

His wife followed him with her sad eyes, with a shade of surprise in them, and answered, "Why, you know, William, she went out with Mr. Rehkopf."

"So much the better, for we have something to talk about."

"What is it? don't keep me in suspense. More trouble? I see it in your face — and through me. What a weight of sorrow I have brought you!"

"Don't say that, Kate. I find that there are troubles yet in store for us, things that I did not expect, but you are not the cause of them as much as I," he continued, in an even, thoughtful tone. "They are the result of what we did years ago. I foresaw then the shadows that would come upon our lives, and they have come, but no thicker nor blacker than I anticipated. We have passed through them together, and the sunshine as well : accepting your condition when I met you as unalterable, I have never wished anything else changed. And you?" he asked, turning quickly to his wife, for he had been speaking in a dreamy tone, with his back toward her, looking into the street.

"Never, William."

"Then never let us spend another moment in useless repinings over what we, with our experi_ ence, would do again. Let us battle with this new disaster, and fight it down as we have so many others. You know I lost sight of your former husband years ago, soon after we left America, in fact. We have long thought him dead, as I could get no information about him, even by the most searching inquiry ; the daughter, too, was lost with him, and you know how, when we believed him dead, I searched for her,

for your sake. We came to this country, believing that the spirit of our past was locked in
our own hearts and in the grave. To-day, after
the board meeting, I strolled up to Hamilton's
room, knocked, and went in. The room was
darkened, and Hamilton sat, spellbound, gazing
at the disk. My presence did not attract his
attention for an instant. I, too, looked at the
disk ; there I saw the naked and emaciated form
of a boy, stretched out rigid and ghostly in the
white light. But a living form stood over him.
I looked in the face of the latter an instant,
then left the room unnoticed. It was the face
of your husband. I could have recognized it
among a million. I can see him now. Pale
and careworn, his deep-sunk eyes glittering
with fire, and the long, white beard, which concealed his face, giving him the appearance of
one of the Magi."

The wife sat limp and motionless, like one
crushed with overwhelming weight, but Van
Rense continued without pause.

"For twenty years I have steeled myself to
meet any terror destiny might have in waiting
for me, and still be unsurprised. Lately, from

want of excitement, I have relaxed my vigilance, and this apparition, arising before me when I least expected it, dazed me. Thank God, Hamilton was too absorbed to notice me, and, after a while, I pulled myself together, and went out. I found out from Wedge that it must have been the inventor, Alder, whom I saw; but nothing more; no one seems to know him, or his family, or where he lives, or whence he came. He has one daughter, however, named Mabel" —

"Mabel," murmured Mrs. Van Rense, softly and sweetly; but otherwise she was too much unnerved to make any other demonstration at this new confirmation of her fears.

"I came away," continued Van Rense, never noticing the interruption, "now cursing myself that I had let my vigilance sleep so soundly as not to have been aroused into carefulness by the name of Alder, for I knew from the first that that was the name of the mysterious inventor; now, sick at heart at finding the same black shadows over our lives as before. But such thoughts are of no use; we must face the music, and take what comes with calmness.

What 's to be done? is the question. I cannot
draw out of my business relations in an instant;
that would hurt my friends, and ruin my own
reputation. On the other hand, out of the—
as we thought—idle dreamer has grown a
giant. Alder is a man of vast powers; the
unknown, mysterious ruler of our company. If
he has not seen and recognized me, he has
friends and intimates among us, who, at some
time or other, will give him a hint. At this
moment he may know all about us, and be
ready to strike. He may be at my elbow,
while to me he is unseen. But come," more
hurriedly, "Laura and Rehkopf have just rid-
den up; smoothe out the terror from your face;
don't let them see it; so, that is better. Now
what is to be done?"

"Be wise for us both, my husband. If my
devotion could only show me a way to help you,
even through death"—

"Never, never say that again, though hell
stare us both in the face!"

The words were sharp and fierce, but they
fell as soft as dew on her feverish heart, lighting
up her face with a tenderness that shone like
sunshine through her falling tears.

But the voices of Laura and Rehkopf were approaching, and Mrs. Van Rense, rising, hurried from the room.

Van Rense turned to the window, trying to compose himself; and he had time, for the two stopped to chat over something in the hall before they came in.

"Good evening, papa," said Laura to her father, going to kiss him. All trace of trouble had vanished from the face and air of the father, as he shook hands with Rehkopf, and asked him about the ride.

"O, we had a pleasant ride," said Rehkopf, who was more interested in Laura than in the jaunt itself.

"Pleasant, indeed! Don't you believe him, papa. It was simply delightful, cool, and lovely. Don't ask him anything about it; he is too practical. Was n't it now superb, Mr. Rehkopf?" It was already arranged, even though they had been acquainted for so short a time, that they were to be married; still, Laura could not quite bring herself to call him Ben, except when no others were by.

"Do you know, Mr. Van Rense, whom Laura

resembles? I was thinking of it when we were riding."

"Something hideous, I suppose," ejaculated that lady.

"Quite the contrary: you remind me of Mabel Alder, the inventor's daughter."

Van Rense gave a start, but no one saw it, the conversation soon turned on other topics, and Laura forgot her resemblance to Mabel in describing a grand old place she had been so greatly taken with on the road.

A grand old manor, covered with ivy, shaded by trees, at one time the home of a large and happy family, but now deserted and falling to ruins, so she thought.

"Where was this stately place?" asked her father, an idea lighting up his face like the reflection from renewed hope.

"'T was just off the old road-agent turnpike," answered Rehkopf, "just beyond the place where, a century ago, a renowned band of highwaymen was surrounded and destroyed to a man. This part of the country was then unpopulated, you know."

"Was there a lake beyond it?" asked Van Rense.

"Yes."

"It must have been the old Van Rense homestead. Would you like to live there, Laura?"

"I should be delighted, papa. It is so hot and noisy here, so cool and quiet there ; we shall go there, shan't we?"

"Your mother and I were speaking of that very thing; how tired we were of all this. By the way, who is this Mabel Alder, — the daughter of the inventor, of course, — but who are they? I confess, the air of mystery with which he surrounds himself piques my curiosity."

"Mr. Alder," said Rehkopf, slowly weighing his words, "is, as I remember him, tall, spare, deep-eyed, gray-bearded, of nervous temperament," —

"Yes, I know," interrupted Van Rense ; "but where does he live?"

"As to that, I can't say. You see, I only saw him once, and that was when we made arrangements to take up his invention. It was evening, too, and more than all that, I was studying possibilities too much to be at liberty to watch for landmarks."

Van Rense saw that he was getting nowhere, and ceased his attack.

" But of Mabel, you say I look like her," said Laura.

" Yes, and she is simply charming," said Rehkopf.

" Oh, now I am jealous," she whispered, but she caught a gleam in Rehkopf's eye that evidently reassured her, and, smiling, she continued, " I wonder if we would be friends; does she have many ? "

" Why, you know her father never goes out, and I do not think that she has even an acquaintance in her own rank in life, except Hamilton and myself, and that's the wonder of it, how she can be as womanly and bright as she was the only time I met her, and have so few opportunities for meeting educated people. Still, so it is, she is simply charming. Hamilton is devoted to her ; and you might be her twin sister except, perhaps, she is a little older, and of dark complexion."

Van Rense left the room and Rehkopf found something more interesting to talk about during the rest of his short stay.

Van Rense's errand was with his wife. He found her in the twilight, her hands clasped before her, and her eyes fixed on space. He stood beside her chair, and there was purpose in his eye and determination in his voice as he said, "I have made up my mind; Laura has just seen our old homestead and is delighted with it. She would like to live there; here, we are in turmoil; there, we could think in quiet. If we were out of people's sight they would cease talking and speculating about us, and, if a crash came, there we would be alone to bear it ; while if it found us here, the whole world would see and magnify it. Besides, if we went there, it would prepare the minds of our friends for a second trip to Europe, where we must go as soon as I can withdraw from my business relations without arousing suspicions. Now I have a knowledge of Alder, and, in the end, will know where to find him. Would it not be better so?"

"You are always wise. I shall be happy wherever you lead me."

He raised her gently from her seat, and, with his arm about her, as in their earliest fortunes, led her to the window.

"What a beautiful sunset we must have had; see how the glow of it lingers into the twilight."

"Yes, my husband, let us take that light as a good omen, for it is bright with the promise of a clear to-morrow."

So let us leave them; though fate glower on them, their devotion to each other is supreme and will endure.

CHAPTER IX.

IN WHICH REHKOPF SEES TROUBLE AHEAD.

REHKOPF, leaving Laura, rode to Hamilton's lodgings. Not finding him there, he hurried to the exchange, hoping to find him in his room. He was successful.

"See here, Al," he cried, on entering, "I have got something to tell you; quit dreaming of Mabel for an instant, and attend to business."

"Well, what is it, Ben?"

"You know the old house in the valley on the road to Alder's; the big, deserted one, I mean?"

"Yes, what of it?"

"It belongs to Van Rense; and, what's more, he is going to fit it up, and move out there."

"Well, what is there startling in that, and what have we got to do with it?"

"Nothing very bad for us, but it will play the mischief with Alder. How long do you suppose it will be, after Van Rense gets out there, before he stores up in his cool head all the facts about the inventor, his life, etc.; then the rest of the directors will know him, and he will have to submit to no end of interviews from them."

"You're right," responded Hamilton, "but how can we help it?"

"I don't know that we can do anything to prevent it, but it looks to me as if the lines were narrowing, and that, despite everything we can do to prevent it, the secret of John Alder's home will soon be in everybody's keeping."

"It must be prevented in some way, if possible," said Hamilton; "it will never do to have him disturbed now."

"Laura and Mabel would be sure to meet, at all events."

"Yes; but you don't see any objection to that, do you?"

"No."

"We can then go from business to pleasure together; sort of a 'birds of a feather,' and so forth."

"These two girls must be related in some way, Al; as I remember Mabel, they look enough alike to be sisters."

"I never thought of that before," said Hamilton, reflectively.

"I have, and a good many times, too; but, of course, it can be nothing but a coincidence," responded Rehkopf.

"Well, never mind that; I have something to tell you of more importance. Alder has discovered a way for renewing youth, — giving life without limit."

"Nonsense!"

"It is the solemn truth, as far as I can judge."

"Bah!"

"Now, don't sneer, Ben, until you hear the whole;" then rising, "but it is getting late; give me time to think it over; meet me here to-morrow, P.M., and I will tell you what I saw through Alder's photo-electrophone, and what the directors thought, when I laid the matter before them. Meanwhile, I am going to Alder's. Shall I say anything about Van Rense's proposed change?"

"No, I think you had better not. Van Rense may possibly not go, and it would be too bad to make Alder's life miserable by anticipation; even if he does move, I think we had better keep the knowledge of it from the old man; he can't help it any."

"By the way, did you notice whether my horse was at the door when you came in?"

"Yes, he was there."

"Let's go, then," and together they descended the stairs, mounted, and rode away.

CHAPTER X.

THE LINES NARROWING.—THE DESERTED HOUSE EXERTS ITS INFLUENCE.

VAN RENSE lost no time in having the old homestead put in order for the reception of his family. Here he could keep quiet, out of the way, lost to sight, and gradually retire from the active business of the Company. Workmen came from far and near; money was poured out like water. Ceiling decorators and cabinet-makers had a merry time of it. National Academicians were impressed into the service by large offers, and, as a result of the decorator's taste and Van Rense's bank account, the old homestead was fitted up with palatial magnificence. With, too, an indescribable air of comfort and a home-like charm; soft-colored ceilings; painted panels; staircases of curiously carved oak; a conservatory as exquisite as a jewel-casket by Benvenuto Cellini; a picture-gallery, which would have aroused the admiration of any art lover. The dining-room was like "that hall, with jewelled windows, in the magical palace which sprang into being in a single night." The walls were upholstered in old gold silk; the curtains, a tawny velvet of deeper tone; cabinets, buffet, and mantels were masterpieces of cabinet work, with high, narrow shelves, and curious recesses holding priceless jars of Oriental enamel. The deep, square hearth was lined and floored with plain, low-toned tiles. No limit was placed upon the expense, everything was to be on the most sumptuous scale. Additions were made to the house in the same quaint style of architecture, giving new and magnificent apartments in carved oak, ebony, and cedar. A library of thousands of volumes, fitted up with every device for comfort and luxurious ease, invited the reader to an intellectual feast.

The whole house was lighted with the new reflected light. Everything that money could buy, which would contribute comfort to this place of comparative solitude, was obtained and utilized.

At last the house was finished, and strangers

came and admired it. Who was to live there, and why they should spend so much money on so isolated a spot, was every one's question; but no answer could be had from either the workmen or the superintendent of the trans- formation.

John Alder's daughter shared with others in the feeling of curiosity as, casting frequent glances into the valley, she saw the old build- ing take on, as if by magic, new and fantastic shapes. The place seemed swarming with workmen, and so rapidly was the work pushed forward, that in a few weeks everything was completed. Meanwhile, thoughts of some com- panionable neighbor, who might come to live there, some one who might be interesting to her, filled her mind. She had spoken of it to her father, but he was too much absorbed in the affairs of the laboratory to do more than cast a hasty look at what had excited her curiosity. She had spoken to Hamilton about it, but he offered no opinion, did not know anything about it, apparently, and would turn the conversation to some other subject.

The family at last arrived, and it soon became

known that a wealthy banker had sought there
retirement from the noise and bustle of life in
the city. As soon as this fact was noised about,
speculation ceased, and, although Van Rense
had been seen by dozens of the town's people
going to and from his home, hardly one of them,
if questioned closely, could have described the
kind of man he was.

For a time everything went along pleasantly.
Van Rense and his wife had supposed that here
they were safe from observation, and had moved
beyond the reach of Alder's influence ; never
suspecting that they had settled almost in his
very presence, and were now in greater danger
of being discovered than ever. Be that as it
may, the family were well pleased with their
surroundings, and, a spirit of contentedness
settling upon them, they looked forward to a
season of quiet happiness in their new home.

CHAPTER XI.

WHAT THE PHYSICIANS SAID.

HAMILTON, faithful to the trust that had been reposed in him by the President and directors of the Company, set to work to find out how the boy progressed upon whom John Alder had wrought so wonderful a change. His every movement was watched by a physician in the employ of the Company, who, with the consent of the boy and his parents, was with him constantly, sharing the same couch. The whole family, physician and all, partook of only such food and water as had been "processed" by John Alder, and agreed, unanimously, that that alone was a wonderful promoter of health.

From time to time the physician made such reports as he deemed necessary, but there was no marked change in them from the first, of which the following is a copy: —

" To MR. ALBIN HAMILTON.

"DEAR SIR, — In obedience to your request,
and with the consent of Philip Thompson, his
wife, and son George — the last of whom you desired me to watch a week ago — I duly installed
myself at his house, where I shall remain until
my services are no longer required. My first
duty was to examine the boy, and make such
memoranda as might be useful in noting any
phenomena which might occur in the future."

The result of the examination was then given
in detail; it consisted in a minute analysis of
the boy's physical condition, such as action of
the heart, temperature, respiration, condition of
tongue, weight, etc., etc. After this statement,
came the general remarks : —

" I find no symptoms of disease about the
lad whatever. He is sound throughout. I can
see no reason why he should not remain so. I
find that the pulse is not accelerated by exer-
cise or excitement. He takes everything coolly,
philosophically. His color is good and healthy.
There has been a slight increase in weight in
the past week, but I see nothing else that I can

enlarge upon at present. I have questioned the parents and the neighbors concerning the previous condition of the boy, and find everything as you stated it to me in the beginning. I hear something about his having been submitted to a process by which disease can wholly be driven out of the system ; but I know and care nothing about that ; the facts are what I have to deal with, and I shall watch narrowly, and note everything."

In another letter, written shortly after, the physician says : "The boy has told me more about the process which I alluded to in my first report to you, and which, at that time, I could do no more than briefly hint at. Day before yesterday, in answer to a few questions, he told me the whole story ; how he was rendered insensible by a certain Mr. Alder ; and also gave a very graphic description of his feelings when restored to consciousness. It is against every theory of the laws of life that-I have ever read or met with ; contrary to the principles which underlie our existence on earth, as they are now accepted. Yet the physical and mental vigor of this boy is an attestation to the fact, that some remarkable change has taken place throughout his entire organization, — a change which is at once important, phenomenal, and beyond my comprehension."

The last and final report from the doctor, after repeating statements with which we are already familiar, said, in conclusion: —

"After carefully reviewing the memoranda made from day to day during the six weeks I have been here with the young man, I have failed to notice any change in him, except in the weight, which has increased only ten pounds altogether; the temperature of the body has always remained the same; no perceptible change in the pulse, sleeping or waking — a most remarkable thing in itself. The boy eats very little, drinks less, and is strong and healthy in every respect, which must be the result of the process; for something must have happened to have produced such a remarkably healthy condition. I do not really see why I should any longer continue to make observations in this case, as there is no noticeable change from one week's end to the other."

On the fourteenth of September, at Hamilton's suggestion, the physician came to the city with the boy, and presented him at a directors' meeting that evening which was held for the purpose of investigating his condition. Friends of the family were also present, and, in the examination which followed, told what they knew concerning the boy's past, and how astonished they had been at the miraculous cure effected by Alder. Expert physicians were also there, specialists in all the ills to which humanity is heir ; each in turn applying his own methods of diagnosis, and all agreeing as to the phenomenally healthy condition of the subject.

The boy himself, when called upon, gave the following simple statement of his feelings: "I was never so well ; no aches, no pains. I used to feel tired always, now I never feel so. I don't get hungry or thirsty either. When the time comes I go to bed ; but when I get up I feel jolly, and as light as a feather. Mr. Alder says I shall live for a hundred years, and not grow old, except in years, and when that time is up, I can go through the process again and live for

another hundred. In short, I am in no danger
of death except by accident, getting crushed,
drowned, blown up, or something of that kind.
I don't know if these things are so; but I
do know that I am not afraid of death as I
used to be, and besides, I have a conviction
that I shall have plenty of time for everything."

At the close of the examination, and after all
but the directors had retired, President Wedge
said : — " Well, gentlemen, you see for yourselves
what shape this latest invention of Alder's is
in; and, from the testimony which has been
offered here, what its future is liable to be. I
think, we should lose no time ; nothing can be
done, however, until we speak with Alder, and
talk him into our way of thinking."

"Then, too," said Hamilton, "I think we
should wait until we see Van Rense and Rehkopf before we determine on anything. I represent Rehkopf, but Van Rense must have been
unavoidably detained."

"Let us, then," said Wedge, "appoint a meeting of the full board for to-morrow evening ; the
night will be the best time to talk with Alder,

and then, every one being present, we shall have the benefit of their ideas."

The meeting then adjourned; but right here it may be well to notice a part of the professional conversation of the doctors as they were leaving. Doctor Stuttsman, a specialist in consumption, was heard to ask the doctor who had been staying with the boy, what he really thought of the case.

"Why," said he, "before that boy passed through that process, he must have had a clear case of slow consumption; no doubt of it, whatever. Is there any consumption about him now?"

"Not in the least," responded Dr. Stuttsman.

"Are there any indications that he will ever be peculiarly subject to it?"

"None whatever — but do you believe in the perpetual life part of the story?"

"O, that's bosh! Alder has solved the great problem of a permanent cure for consumption, that's the amount of it; and then, again, the food that the boy eats, prepared in the way in which it is, has a great deal to do with his present appearance and health."

This was, in all essential details, the common opinion of all the professional men present at the examination. They were the most noted men in their profession, in that section of the country at least, if not in the whole. Their opinion, consequently, was of great weight. If we are to accept the conclusions of these scientists, it is evident that Alder must have been mentally deranged and jumped at conclusions, to which methods of procedure his whole former life and attainments are in direct opposition.

CHAPTER XII.

AT THE CLIFFS.—THE FACE IN THE CLOUDS.

THE same evening, which was a little over a week after the Van Rense family had moved to their country-seat, Mabel and her father were sitting in the same observation place where we last saw them together. All this time Mabel had seen but little of her father, and knew nothing about his work. Before that visit of Hamilton, a little over two months ago, Mabel had been accustomed to sit in the laboratory to read, or work, or even help her father while he experimented ; had been accustomed to hear him talk of his plans and his success ; but of late, whenever she went into his room, her father showed a spirit of annoyance, and would take but little or no notice of her, and, in the few times when the intercourse of the household brought them together, he showed no inclination to talk. Often, while at the table, he, leaving his food untouched, would slip away into moody silence, and sit there, a weary look in his face, which Mabel had not seen there for many years.   It was not long before the change in her father struck her as something alarming, and her mind, acted upon by her lonely life, now that he kept so much to himself, dwelt upon it as a most serious matter.   At first, she did not know what was the cause of it, but she soon concluded that it must be her approaching marriage with Hamilton, and had already made up her mind to speak with her father, to give up her future for his sake.   But, totally unexpected, her father appeared this evening on the observation place, where she sat alone, and showed a disposition to return to his former habits.   She suppressed all surprise at the event, and turned her attention to a conversation that, by interesting him in this or that, should have a tendency to draw him out of his contemplative state of mind.   In the conversation, they drifted finally to the house in the valley, and Mabel called the name of the gentleman who lived there; but it made no apparent impression on Alder.

Later on, when it had grown darker, Alder brought out the hand-reflector before mentioned, and silently amused himself by throwing the light far and near, now lighting up some distant hill or farmhouse miles away, now throwing it on the clouds, where a brilliant spot of light appeared. To Mabel, as she sat watching the effect, an idea suddenly occurred; it was to use this new invention as a means for communication. She mentioned it to her father, ran into the house, found an old negative of her father's face, which she brought out and held in front of the reflector. The effect was instantaneous, and the gigantic face of Alder, as in his youthful days, appeared on the clouds.

Mabel was delighted at first, but on looking at her father and seeing his head sink, she felt that she had hurt his feelings in some way, calling up recollections of his youth, that past of which he never had spoken, and had forbidden her to question him about.

"Forgive me, father," she cried, hastily drawing back her hand. "I did n't mean it; I am so sorry. Let us look at something else."

The old man raised his head; the face in the

clouds had disappeared, but, without looking in
that direction, he lowered the light to the land
and allowed it to wander aimlessly about, until,
at Mabel's suggestion, it settled on the Van
Rense mansion. Here it rested for a while,
lighting up every nook and corner, making every
bit of furniture on the veranda or in the gar-
dens distinctly visible.

Alder gazed indifferently for a moment, when
Mabel said, "That must be Mr. Van Rense
and his wife out there; they seem to be disturbed about something. I wonder what they
are doing."

"What!" cried Alder, greatly excited, dropping the reflector suddenly, and rushing into the
house.

In a moment Mabel saw him come hurrying
back, bringing in his hand a piece of tracing
paper, which he placed before the reflector, after
turning it once more to the clouds.

Mabel knew not what to make of her father's
actions, and for the first time doubts of his
sanity dawned upon her.

CHAPTER XIII.

IN THE VALLEY.—VAN RENSE AND HIS ENEMY FACE TO FACE.

LET us turn now to the Van Renses and mark the effect of John Alder's power upon them. As had been their custom in the few days past at their new home, Mr. Van Rense and his wife were sitting on a kind of balcony, looking toward the Cliffs, enjoying the cool of the evening.

The heat had been oppressive during the day, and, as the sun went down, heavy banks of clouds appeared in the northeast, which, gradually spreading over the sky, gave every indication of a storm. But, though the black pall settled densely over the earth, it brought with it no sign of wind, and the heat became almost unbearable.

"What's that?" suddenly asked Mrs. Van Rense of her husband, as she pointed to a bright pencil of light from the Cliffs, that was moving in a mysterious way over the country.

" I have n't the slightest idea," responded the husband. " I was watching the same thing ; at other times I have seen other things that struck me as a little queer, to say the least. Night before last, while I was out here alone, I saw great points of flame shoot up from that very spot; and this morning, at the station, I overheard some people talking about a queer genius who lives up there, some one who is continually at work upon some new plan to perform great things. But I heard nothing particular, however."

" Heavens! what is that?" cried Mrs. Van Rense, starting from her chair, and directing her husband's attention to the semblance of a face on the low, hanging clouds. Above them, in the clouds, hung the face of John Alder, as he was twenty years ago, but, to their imagination, the eyes seemed to burn with a fierce, unquenchable fire.

" John Alder!" exclaimed Van Rense. " At last, I have found him."

" The very clouds are his!" moaned his

wife. "He will find us out, even here. Oh, God, he knows it now!"

But the picture in the clouds quickly disappeared, and the light again wandered aimlessly over the country.

"Look! it is coming this way," she cried, as she saw the light coming toward the homestead.

"Yes, he is now, even now, looking at us," exclaimed Van Rense, as the light paused over the house, lighting it up in a blaze of glory.

Mrs. Van Rense covered her face with her hands, while her husband stood beside her chair, his head bowed; a picture of utter dejection.

"This is too much!" he cried at last, angrily.

Instantly the light vanished, and, for a few moments there was no new cause of disturbance. Van Rense had begun to feel that it was all over, when, suddenly, his wife gave a startled cry, and sprang from her chair, only to fall prostrate upon the floor of the balcony.

Van Rense looked up; nothing could have startled him more. Upon the clouded sky, in letters of gigantic proportions, appeared:—

"I watch while you sleep.
Your sins shall find you out."

"Oh, God! God!" moaned the prostrate wife; "we are lost! lost!"

The effect upon Van Rense was magical. All traces of gloom and fear forsook him, and there came in their stead determination and consciousness of duty. He lifted his prostrate wife and bore her into the house. Once having brought her to her room, he hastened to administer restoratives, taking care, however, to draw no one's attention to the scene. He succeeded perfectly in escaping observation; but his wife remained unconscious for so long a time, that he, even with his knowledge of her, began to be alarmed. He was on the point of summoning assistance, when she showed signs of returning consciousness. He renewed his exertions, and soon had the satisfaction of seeing her rouse herself, and a gleam of intelligence come into her eyes.

"There, Kate; don't be alarmed; the worst is over; we know the worst, except the final evil. But come, let us talk of something else."

"No! this suspense is killing me! what can we do?"

"Perhaps you're right, Kate, but first we must

prepare ourselves for exposure and disgrace; fortune may help us as she has done before, but there is no longer any use in hiding from Alder. John Alder knows us, and has a power to reach us wherever we may go. If help there be, it is in ourselves, in what Alder intends to do, in our power to prevent or change it. I am going to see him, and soon; to-morrow night, I think. I will see him; it will do us no harm, and in such an interview I shall have every advantage. I will worm from him what he intends doing. I will change his purpose if I can; if not, we shall be prepared, knowing what's to come. As it is, we may live on here for days, fearful and trembling, in the expectation of something that may never arrive."

But Mrs. Van Rense was not so easily convinced; she was afraid for her husband, afraid for his life, if he should once cross the threshold of the mysterious power on the Cliffs. She would rather draw each breath in fear than miss him from her side. Against his resolution, therefore, she pleaded, her voice trembling and full of tears. But it was weak and faint, while his was strong and resolute, yielding nothing.

Gradually there came a calm, and, in the end, slumber, fitful or peaceful, settled both on the dwellers at the Cliffs and in the valley, John Alder alone excepted.

He, through the long, still watches of the night, followed, with eager, anxious gaze, the course of certain daring experiments, compounding this, reducing that, gathering and concentrating the most powerful forces of nature into little space. So he toiled with nervous energy, and, indeed, with a different method than ever before; then it was with care and appreciation for the means employed; now careless of the interesting side of what was immediately going forward, he was watching and working with impatience for a result. Many a time, as Van Rense lay tossing between the dozes, he saw the gigantic shadow of Alder on the clouds, cast there through the open space in the laboratory roof, by the fierce furnace fires over which he was bending.

CHAPTER XIV.

AT THE CLIFFS.—JOHN ALDER ALONE.—THE APPROACHING STORM.

The evening of the next day, the fifteenth of September, also proved hot and sultry for that time of the year; the promised storm of the preceding evening had not come to pass, and now the air was heavy and charged with electricity. The setting sun had disappeared in a cloud; the twilight brought a heavy stillness, broken now and then by hot breezes, which rustled the leaves, and turned their light sides to the sky.

The house of Alder, always very quiet, was now unwontedly still. Mabel was away from home; the old servant was dozing in one of Mabel's hammocks; away off on the horizon, the vanguard of a storm appeared, growing fast and dark. In this most dismal part of the day, rendered doubly melancholy by the sultry stillness and fast-approaching storm, Alder, in his workshop, toils and toils, — a different man, mentally, at least, from him who, two months or so ago, threw the light from his reflector into Hamilton's face, as he galloped up the road to the Cliffs. What caused the change?

At the formation of the Photo-electrophone Company, or very soon thereafter, Alder found himself free from care, and supplied with a sufficiency of money to carry out his wildest ambition. He immediately took up, or rather renewed that pet idea of his youth, namely, the prolongation of life; and, though he accomplished no great results in this new field for his inventive ability, a season of quiet happiness followed, to the like of which he had been a stranger since the early part of his married life.

But to this pleasant state of affairs there came an end, and a rude one, too. Suddenly he found Van Rense, the old enemy of his happiness, the destroyer of his home, at his side; profiting, as director of the Company, by his toil and brains. That knowledge took away every happy moment from his life; his old misery was

renewed. No matter how forgiving a spirit he
cherished toward his wife, he knew that he had
been wronged. Now, he saw her and her husband happy and prosperous, nay, even taking
greater advantage of him, while he knew that
he himself was miserable.

But how could he change it? He must think,
but he could hit on no plan; in his thoughts he
found no comfort; they became a terror to him,
and he fled from them to his work. The passion,
for it grew on him, absorbed his time by day
and night, and sapped his strength. Daily he
became more and more nervous; last night, he
resolved to break from the mental confusion to
which harassing thoughts, incessant toil, and
sleepless nights had brought him, and he renewed his old-time custom of an evening *siesta*
with Mabel. But even here he found a blacker,
a more awful reminder of his misfortune than
ever before; though he did not notice Mabel's
first remark about the inhabitants of the house
in the valley, when he came to look there and
heard the hated name again, it dawned upon
him like an instantaneous, overwhelming shock.
His soul cried out within him, "Let me kill

them! let me terrify them!" He rushed into the house for the paper.

How he succeeded we already know, but that was the end; like an expiring torch he could give out now and then a fitful lurid glare, but that was all. Now, though he saw his old enemy near, almost at his very hearthstone, though he knew himself rich and powerful, still he was incapable of sitting quietly down to develop any definite plan for righting himself, and he knew it ; for was he not unacquainted with the world, afraid of men and their talk, and, loving his daughter, wishing to shield her from all ill-repute ?

How careful he had been all his life, never to enter into any project that would have a tendency to draw him into contact with men. Yet, within the last two months, he had done all he could to make that care of no avail. He had given his consent to his daughter's marriage, and the result of that in this direction would be certain. The doctor had been located in a neighboring village, with his consent, to watch over the boy, and now necessarily knew all about him. Then, supposing the apparent success of the latest invention proved in time a failure, had he not accepted in two short months, as a fact, something which a generation of time alone could prove; something which was a huge advance over anything that he had gained in all the former years of toil and study. Suppose this was wrong; what a whirlwind of reproach, both from himself and from the men who now believed in him, would rage over his head if he ever came into the mental position to notice it.

This phase of the question never had presented itself to him; thoughts of Van Rense and his wife were dominant in his mind. Through them he saw the rising world-tide surrounding his life, as a flood might surround the lonely eminence where he lived, sweeping nearer and nearer; no escape, and with cold sweat and trembling he imagined a time rushing toward him with headlong speed, when he should find himself struggling on its surface; when his private life, himself, and his daughter would be paraded before the world, and his impotency made plain. This was weak and foolish, we know, but, in his diseased mind, his ability, power, and wealth passed for nothing, while the shame that seemed to hang over him was all-absorbing.

It is not, therefore, the quiet, contented, studious man of former times who stands here in the laboratory, in the growing darkness and storm, but one over-wrought, half-crazed, supported by frenzy. But now the nervous excitement culminates; familiar objects take on strange shapes and dance about him. Terrified, perhaps for the first time in his life, he flees from what had been his only refuge. Outside of the laboratory he gropes about like one blind.

"Mabel, Mabel!" he calls, sharp, quick, as in agony. He gets no answer; he falls faint into a chair.

"Alone, alone! how weak and ill I feel. Is this the end?" with a shudder. "Oh, Kate, that you had been more patient with me. Why, why, oh God! do I live in torment, while he—? She was too young. I thought she loved me; I did not know, how could I know, the monotony of her existence? But Van Rense! O God! keep me from myself; crush me beneath a greater load of sorrow, if it be possible, but not this, not this; let me die! let me die! sober and calm, I pray. I, who could not know of love, should not have married; she should not have fled me; how my head throbs. I shall go mad: but no, I will be calm, and loose the forces that shall shake the earth."

With a mighty effort the old man stood erect, drew his cold and nerveless fingers once or twice across his eyes, as if to banish some hideous dream, then staggered back into the laboratory.

Outside the storm was raging; the winds howled and tugged at the old building as if to sweep it into the lake below; but the play of the lightning about the lonely spot, the heavy crash and roar of heaven's artillery, passed unheeded by John Alder, who, roused once more to frenzy by the spirit of his work, was bending all his wavering energies on some new and grand experiment.

CHAPTER XV.

IN WHICH THE READER SEES THE DIRECTORS FOR
THE LAST TIME, AND THE DISK INTRODUCES A
SERIOUS MATTER.

AT the time of the events narrated in the last
chapter, the directors were already assembled in
the Company's rooms to discuss the possibilities
and prospects of Alder's latest discovery, which
was to give to humanity a new hold upon the
things of earth. There was no doubt in their
minds that Alder and the invention could ac-
complish what had been promised. They knew
nothing of Alder's changed state of mind, and
supposed that the invention was the result of a
gradual, logical advance, every step of which
had been watched and investigated, for and
against. All their previous connection with Alder and what they knew of his method of work
led them naturally to this conclusion. A feeling,
therefore, of unrest, of anxiety to organize a

company, and to get its affairs into working order, so that they might be benefited personally by the invention, was visible in the faces of all.

The President glanced at his watch from time to time, and finally, an hour after the time set for the meeting, called the board to order.

"Gentlemen!" said he, "I do not see why we should wait any longer for Messrs. Van Rense and Rehkopf; they are already an hour late, so, if you please, we will proceed without them, and try to deal equitably with them afterwards. But before we call up John Alder, perhaps it would be better to arrange our own ideas into one plan, so that, if he accedes to it, he may be spared details, for which he has always shown a decided aversion. Any suggestions or remarks are now in order; the meeting is in your hands."

Silence pervaded the room for a moment, then Hamilton arose and said : —

"Mr. President, this invention is the crowning effort of Alder's life. He has virtually put it, as you see, into our hands to manage. If I know the man and his character at all, he con-

siders his part performed, and would be willing
to accede to almost any plan we might make.
He places implicit confidence in us. Now the
question is, whether we shall take advantage of
the trust he reposes in us, and get the best bar-
gain possible for ourselves, or whether we shall
yield to him willingly what another man of more
business training would fight for and undoubtedly get. He has already, in giving us control
of perpetual sunlight, made us rich; and it
seems to me, that we ought to be willing that
he should hold one-quarter interest in this invention." He sat down.

John Wedge said: — "If we had absolute
control of the whole process, if there was no
part of it that remained unrevealed to us, I
should most heartily agree to such a proposition. In so far as the process applies to the
preservation of meat, it is well enough and
there is money in it ; but when we come to
apply it to the living human body, what if Alder
refuses to give up the secret of the anæsthetic?"

"Let us call him and see," said Bruce.

The directors then turned their attention to
the disk. Hardly had they taken in the details

of the scene before them, when an exclamation of surprise came from the lips of all.

There, in the centre of the laboratory, partly stooping over a large trap in the floor, stood John Alder, intently watching some process going on below. There was noise of hissing and straining, as if a pent-up power were struggling for release from bands that were confining it.

Suddenly a bright red light, from below, lit up the face of the chemist with a weird, fantastic glow. His eyes glistened, his hands opened and shut convulsively, his gaunt, spare frame trembled, apparently with anxiety over the result of his experiment.

The noise grew louder and louder, the disk vibrating with the sound until it seemed as if it could no longer withstand the power that controlled it. The light grew brighter and glowed with fiercer intensity. They saw the chemist start and stretch out his hands, as if to grasp something below him, when there came a flash of dazzling brilliancy, a sharp, bursting sound, as if the furies could no longer be withstood, — then all was blank.

"What could it mean? Something awful had happened; what was the solution of the scene?" the excited directors asked of one another in the darkness. Perhaps Hamilton could explain. They turned on the light and looked for him. He was gone.

"A serious matter this," they said.

CHAPTER XVI.

THE STORM; IN WHICH MABEL MEETS HER MOTHER AND THE LIGHT ON THE CLIFFS GOES OUT.

ALL this time Mabel Alder was away from the Cliffs. Just before sundown she had started off for a ride, but an hour had not passed before the indications of a coming storm became so positive that she turned about and urged on her horse, hoping to reach home before the storm should break; already stray drops of enormous proportions were falling about her, an earnest of a deluge to come.

As she clattered along the road approaching the neighborhood of the Van Rense house, two other riders, a man and a woman, came at a gallop out of a wood-path a rod or so in advance of her. The man, looking back, recognized Mabel. It was Rehkopf. His companion was Laura Van Rense. These two held up their horses until Mabel joined them, and a hurried introduction took place as they galloped along in company.

"These drops mean business," said Rehkopf.

"Yes, but we are nearly home, now; but what will you do, Miss Alder?"

"Oh, I shall be home before the worst comes."

"You will get drenched; you have at least another mile to go; you cannot think of it. Look! it is raining up there now," said she, pointing in the direction of the Cliffs, already obscured by the falling rain.

"Come in with us until it blows over, or until we can order the carriage."

"That's the wisest thing you can do, Miss Alder," urged Rehkopf. "I will see that you get safely back when the tempest is over. Your father will not be anxious."

"Oh, no; he is very busy at this hour, and even if I were at home I should not see him until nine or ten in the evening."

"Then you will come in, will you not?" said Laura.

"You will have to give the horses freer rein or we shall catch it, as it is," exclaimed Rehkopf, giving his horse the spur.

His companions followed suit; the conversation stopped. At the entrance to the avenue leading up to the house they all turned in and sped along the smooth, broad pathway, under majestic oaks, which were already groaning and creaking under the fierce blasts of wind.

Mrs. Van Rense, the mother of these two young ladies, still was standing at the window from which she had, a quarter of an hour ago, watched her husband out of sight on his way to meet Alder at the Cliffs. She was watching the hurrying clouds and lurid flashes of lightning, unconscious of terror, for her own heart was in a turmoil with which the tempest in the air was in accord. Recollections of the long ago, consciousness of the present, her husband's danger, the uncertain outcome of his visit, and the dark fate hanging over her, were all at work on her sensitive nature, playing on her heartstrings a terrific tune.

After her husband disappeared from sight came the lull in the air, when the birds hush their song,—that calm so full of wind. Then came the roaring tempest, the falling darkness, and the pattering rain. Out from the shadows of the avenue dashed the three riders, and drew up at the door.

Mrs. Van Rense noticed that there were three, and that the stranger was a woman; this fact, fitting in with the reveries of that lady, filled her with forebodings. She knew, before she met the party, that the stranger was her first child, the little two-year-old Mabel, whom she deserted twenty years ago. She made up her mind to the part she must play as well as she could, and went to meet them.

Downstairs the servants had turned on the light, and all was cheerful; no hint of the storm anywhere, except in the mind of Mrs. Van Rense, who held in her imagination the scene being enacted on the Cliffs in the midst of the thunder and the lightning.

In the hall-way stood the three young people, shaking the water from their clothing, and gaily joking at the mischance that had thrown them so unexpectedly together.

Mrs. Van Rense appeared.

"This is Miss Mabel Alder, mother, whom we have been so anxious to meet," said Laura.

Remembrances of the tenderness she had felt

for this daughter, hopes of happiness that had come at her birth, stirred the mother's heart; resolution vanished like a dream. "Mabel!" she murmured; 't was all she dared say; and her eyes were bright with unshed tears as she took her to her heart as a daughter.

No one except Rehkopf noticed anything peculiar in this sudden display of affection; and he, though remembrances of it clung to him for years, never could satisfactorily explain it. Mabel herself was too new to the world to be surprised at the warmth of her reception. Knowing instinctively that it was heartfelt, she returned it, and glided easily into a relationship which grew closer and closer with time.

Mrs. Van Rense dared say nothing; she was afraid her emotion would betray itself in her voice; the silence was becoming painful, when a burst of thunder shook the house.

"What a storm," said Laura. "Hear the rain; how it pours."

"Yes," said Mabel, turning towards her; "but don't you like to see it?"

"No; do you?"

"Yes; when I'm at home, and such storms

come up, I like to climb as high as I can in the
house, and, while its old rafters creak and groan
at every burst of the wind, watch the boiling
lake, and the tossing trees below me; or follow
the dense columns of rain as they sweep across
the valley, over the hills, and far away. Then
I see the workings of God's great forces. I
feel myself a part of them, and at home; but "—
a shadow of sadness coming into her face, as
she added—"sometimes very lonely."

"Lonely, poor child ; what a dreary place it
must be for you, up there between heaven and
earth," said Mrs. Van Rense, looking toward
the Cliffs, for they had all accepted Mabel's
idea, and were now at a window, watching the
storm.

"Yes, lonely, but never sad," said Mabel.
"You know I have never known any other life,
and at such times I seem to be so near to the
powers of nature that I feel my heart swell as
I note the grandeur of them. Then, too, while
I am watching from my tower, I think of my
father, working below me, handling these awful
forces like babies' toys."

"You are your father's child," said Mrs. Van

Rense, without thinking; then hastily recollect-
ing herself — "but your father; does he never
watch with you?"

"He used to," replied Mabel, "but then sel-
dom, for he was always very busy; lately he has
been much more occupied than ever — so much
so, that sometimes I am afraid for him. There
was a time when he used to tell me of his success, and explain it to me; but now, for months,
some new, absorbing idea has held him, and he
applies himself so seriously that" —

A blinding flash of light, and a strange,
frightful noise startled them: not long and
echoing like the thunder, but sharp and quick.
Trembling, they looked about for the cause.
They were still more startled when Mabel,
straining her eyes through the darkness, cried,
in agony, "Look! look! my father's light —
where is it? Something has happened; I know
it! I feel it! The light is out!" Turning, she
tried to hurry from the room, but trembling,
friendly hands stopped her.

Mrs. Van Rense had fallen fainting into a
chair in the darkness, overcome by her own
dread and the prophetic words of her child.

Laura and Rehkopf, unconscious of her, were uniting their strength to stop Mabel, who seemed determined to rush aimlessly out into the storm, trying to reassure her.

"Mabel," said Rehkopf, forgetting ceremony in his excitement, "you wait here: this is no season for you to be out in. Keep her fast, Laura; my horse is still saddled; I'll find out what has happened. Don't be frightened, Mabel; I feel sure it is nothing bad. You shall know it all in a few moments; till then keep up your courage, and stay here: it is the best place."

He hurried away, and the two girls found plenty of occupation for their distracted thoughts in restoring their mother to consciousness.

CHAPTER XVII.

IN WHICH THE STORM INCREASES, AND THE DIF-
FERENCES BETWEEN ALDER AND VAN RENSE
ARE SETTLED FOR ALL TIME. — FIVE YEARS
LATER.

MEANWHILE Van Rense was on his way to
the Cliffs, on foot and alone, to determine, if
possible, the purposes of John Alder. The
storm, which had been brewing for days, was
now upon him. The wind blew in fitful gusts,
the rain had commenced to fall. Great, angry,
copper-colored clouds rolled on above him.
Nothing daunted, Van Rense pushed on,
resolved that this night should settle for all
time all differences existing between himself
and Alder. Harder and harder blew the wind;
fiercer and sharper grew the glare of the lightning; louder and nearer rolled the thunder;
great trees bowed their heads in meek submis-
sion to the tempest's wrath; the air was filled

with leaves and branches fleeing before the driving gale. It was an appalling scene, but Van Rense wavered not ; he could not go back. The storm was behind him ; he would go on, he must go on. A sharp bend in the road, as he started with renewed courage to ascend the hill, brought the full force of the storm in his face. The rain, which was now falling in blinding torrents, made it impossible for him to see his way before him. A blast of wind, more fearful than all the rest, threw a huge tree across the road. He could not go forward ; the very elements forbade his further progress. But where should he go, where rest until the storm was over ?

The tree when it fell had torn up with its matted roots masses of earth and mould, which now, rising like a wall, offered protection against the storm. Here Van Rense took his station, and, peering out from behind this shelter, looked up to the Cliffs and watched the bright lights from Alder's windows' beaming through the rain.

But there were new terrors in store for him. A low, rumbling sound, as if coming from the heart of the Cliffs, and heard above the roar and battle of the elements, shook the earth. A wild hissing and screaming, more terrible than anything he had ever heard before, filled the air. Louder and louder it grew; then an explosion of terrific force threw up a fountain of fire, hurling aloft great masses of dazzling light, which, mingling with the vivid lightning, illumined hilltop and plain for miles around. Sprays, points, and arrows of flame, edged with a perfect glory of lesser lights, soared higher and higher, fading from sight. Crash succeeded crash from the heavens; then dead stillness and darkness.

The storm had reached its climax and was now subsiding. Van Rense, terror-stricken, by force of will, dragged himself slowly up the hill; the rain was still falling; the violence of the wind was little abated, but this was of no moment to him now.

As he toiled on, his eyes fixed unwaveringly on the Cliffs, a flash of lightning showed it empty and barren. Alder's house had disappeared. John Alder himself was no more.

Van Rense at last arrived on the scene of the explosion. All his private troubles were forgotten in the awe that filled him when he thought of the fate of Alder. The house had entirely disappeared, not a splinter remained; where it had stood the earth was torn out, leaving a hole, broad, ragged, and deep. He half suspected that Alder and his surroundings had been a product of his imagination, for he and his dwelling had vanished into air, leaving no "wrack behind." His own troubles grew quiet and settled, as he stood there motionless; he had no respect for Alder outside of his inventive sphere. He saw the only obstacle to his perfect happiness removed, and by no doings of his own. Then the thought dawned upon him that perhaps the explosion was some miscalculated means for his own destruction. He grew pale and trembled at the danger he had escaped.

He heard the sharp ring of horses' hoofs approaching, and Rehkopf appeared upon the plateau.

Each told the other what he knew; Van Rense giving the full particulars of the explosion, and Rehkopf telling what had been seen from the valley, — where Mabel was, and how she had said that her father must certainly be at work.

Together they descended into the pit and groped about in the darkness, rain, and wind, for a clew to the mischance, a token of Alder: but they found nothing. Every trace had vanished ; the cavity was as clean as though newly dug.

After a time they turned their backs on the scene of the explosion, and in silence departed homeward, each busy with his own thoughts.

Van Rense had witnessed an awful scene of destruction. The shadow of death seemed spread over him still. He felt lost. He could not consider it in any personal light; still he acknowledged to himself, in his heart, a feeling of relief. No more hiding. That other shadow which had blackened his life for twenty years had vanished. The skeleton in his closet had been put away. At last ! at last !

Rehkopf never had an idea of the thoughts which were occupying the mind of his companion. He was the prey of sadness. Mabel was awaiting him in the valley. What must he say to her? How could he lessen the shock?

Van Rense at his house found everything in disorder; his wife unconscious, and the two girls at their wits' end. Mabel had already made up her mind regarding the accident at the Cliffs, and the report she would hear from it. When Rehkopf told her what had happened she accepted the realization of her fears with calmness, but, after the excitement, she was not herself for many days.

An hour afterward, Hamilton, hatless and drenched, galloped up to the house. He saw that there was no longer any light on the Cliffs, and his heart sank within him, for he, too, knew what must have happened. But he supposed that Mabel had shared in the disaster. He could not go on, he was sick and faint. Turning in to the Van Rense homestead, he drew rein at the door, fell rather than descended from his saddle, and staggered into the house, expecting to find there the confirmation of his worst fears.

He learned at once that Mabel was there and

safe. He saw her ; with tears she told him all that had happened.

FIVE YEARS LATER.

On the fifth anniversary of the destruction of John Alder and his home on the Cliffs, Hamilton and his family and Rehkopf and his family again visited the spot made famous by that disaster.

These five years the two families had spent in travelling over the world in company, and now, on their return, visit the Cliffs together.

There, in the centre of a broad, ragged rent in the rocky earth, once covered by Mabel's home, stood a rough granite shaft which Mabel had caused to be erected to the memory of her father.

At the top of the shaft a powerful reflector, one of her father's latest inventions, was placed. This reflector was connected with one of the great central illuminating lines, and so arranged that its rays were directed vertically.

Each night the sunlight from all parts of the earth was hurried to this spot, a tribute to the great inventor's memory ; and the superstitious dwellers in the country round about declared, that many a time, when the storm-clouds hung low, and the pillar of light tried in vain to penetrate them, they had seen, hovering near the bright spot in the clouds, the wild, weird face of John Alder.

www.ingramcontent.com/pod-product-compliance
Lightning Source LLC
Chambersburg PA
CBHW020626030726
47497CB00007B/2439